For more than forty years,
Yearling has been the leading name
in classic and award-winning literature
for young readers.

Yearling books feature children's
favorite authors and characters,
providing dynamic stories of adventure,
humor, history, mystery, and fantasy.

Trust Yearling paperbacks to entertain,
inspire, and promote the love of reading
in all children.

OTHER YEARLING BOOKS YOU WILL ENJOY

TROUBLE DON'T LAST, *Shelley Pearsall*

CROOKED RIVER, *Shelley Pearsall*

STEALING FREEDOM, *Elisa Carbone*

STORM WARRIORS, *Elisa Carbone*

THE TRIAL, *Jen Bryant*

JOSHUA T. BATES TAKES CHARGE, *Susan Shreve*

THE FLUNKING OF JOSHUA T. BATES, *Susan Shreve*

DEAR LEVI: LETTERS FROM THE OVERLAND TRAIL
Elvira Woodruff

DEAR AUSTIN: LETTERS FROM
THE UNDERGROUND RAILROAD
Elvira Woodruff

INTO THE

Firestorm

A Novel of San Francisco, 1906

DEBORAH HOPKINSON

A YEARLING BOOK

Published by Yearling, an imprint of Random House Children's Books
a division of Random House, Inc., New York

Cover title lettering by Iskra Johnson

Cover photograph, a detail of "Looking east on Market Street from 4th [i.e., Fourth]
and Stockton Streets. April 18, 1906. :70," reproduced with permission of the
Bancroft Library, University of California, Berkeley, Roy D. Graves Pictorial Collection.

Visit us on the Web! www.randomhouse.com/kids

Educators and librarians, for a variety of teaching tools, visit us at
www.randomhouse.com/teachers

ISBN: 978-0-440-42129-0

Reprinted by arrangement with Alfred A. Knopf Books for Young Readers

Printed in the United States of America

March 2008

10 9 8 7

First Yearling Edition

*To Maya, Stewart, and Ruby
(who, like Shake, is a very good dog),*

and special thanks to the real Nick

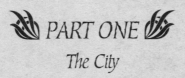# PART ONE
The City

That night it seemed to me that
fun-loving San Francisco was
merrier than ever. . . .

—Harry Coleman,
photographer for the
San Francisco Examiner, 1906

ROAD KID

"Hey, kid. Get back here and empty your pockets."

Nicholas Dray whirled to see a burly policeman pointing a black club right at him. He froze in astonishment. This should not be happening. Not to Nick the Invisible.

Nick could count only three things he was good at. First, he could pick cotton. Working cotton—planting, thinning, chopping the weeds away with a hoe, and picking—was about all he'd done for most of his eleven years.

Nick wasn't bad at writing, either. Oh, not putting words together to tell a story or anything, just making letters and words look nice. Back in Texas, he would often come home after working in the fields and sink down with his back against their wooden shack. Before long he'd be scratching in the dust with a stick until Pa yelled at him to finish his chores or Gran called him in to eat some steaming-hot corn bread.

Being invisible was Nick's third and newest skill. He'd only gotten good at it since becoming a road kid, since that morning a few weeks ago when he'd finally taken off from the Lincoln Poor Farm for Indigents and Orphans.

Nick had worried a lot about whether he'd be able to make it to California from Texas. But between begging rides from farmers and even hopping a few freight trains, things had gone pretty well. Not one policeman or official-looking person had paid him any mind. In fact, Nick had gotten so confident, he'd begun to think of himself as Nick the Invisible.

So how could he have let this policeman sneak up on him? How could it be that now, when he'd finally arrived in San Francisco, just where he wanted to be, he wasn't invisible at all?

"Hey, kid, didn't you hear me the first time? Get back here and empty your pockets." The policeman's yell drowned out the clanking of a cable car. The big man lumbered closer, looking like a giant bear, with bushy red eyebrows sprouting every which way. "I saw you stick your grimy hand into that vegetable cart."

"You can't send me back. I didn't take anything, Bushy Brows," Nick mumbled out loud, pushing off into a run.

And that was true enough. Nick hadn't stolen a thing—at least not yet. He'd only stopped to feast his eyes on the bright lettuces and cabbages and breathe in the fresh, sweet scent of oranges piled in neat rows. He couldn't help it. He was that hungry.

Nick pulled his old brown cap over his curly hair and lunged into the crowd. His wild hair could be a problem. It made him easy to spot—and made it easy for policemen like Bushy Brows to remember him.

Nick never used to mind his hair. For one thing, Gran kept it cut close during cotton season so as to keep his head cooler. She'd always told Nick his hair was a gift from his mother. Since his mother had died when he was born, Nick didn't carry any real memories of her, not the kind that make you sad, anyway. There was just that faded wedding photograph in a cracked frame that Gran kept free of dust as best she could.

5

"My, how Janet would've laughed to see such a shock of wild curls wasted on a boy," Gran would say in her soft drawl as Nick sat on an upturned bucket while she trimmed away. She always made sure to scatter the cut locks to the wind so the birds would have something for their nests.

Nick risked a glance back at the policeman. Another mistake. He wheeled forward again to find a well-dressed man with a thick brown mustache barreling down on him.

At that moment, Bushy Brows let loose an ear-splitting cry. "Stop. Thief!"

"A thief, eh? I'll teach you, young ruffian," growled the man, thrusting out a long black umbrella.

Crack!

"Ow!" Nick cried out as the umbrella hit his shins. The man made a grab for him, but Nick twisted away, his heart pounding. His head felt light from not eating.

Nick did his best, though. He skipped around businessmen in suits and hats, ladies in long dark skirts and crisp white shirtwaist blouses, deliverymen toting crates and boxes. Veering onto the cobblestone street to avoid bumping a tottering elderly lady, he found himself face to face with a snorting horse pulling a cart.

"Easy, Betsy," the driver crooned to his mare. "You watch it, boy. Lucky for you I ain't driving one of those fast new automobiles."

By now Nick was panting. He could feel drops of sweat trickle down the back of his neck. This should have been easy, but everything was going wrong. And then, just when he felt sure he'd left the police officer behind, he tripped.

Nick threw out his hands, scraping his palms hard on the sidewalk. He groaned and closed his eyes, feeling a wave of sickness wash over him. It all sounded far away: laughter and voices, the ironclad wheels of wagons clattering along on cobbled streets, cable cars screeching and clanging.

"I got you." Nick felt something hard jab into his back.

The large, round officer loomed above him, panting slightly. Nick looked up and tried to bring the man into focus. His eyebrows were enormous, with hairs sticking out in all directions like a thicket of blackberry branches.

The officer poked. "Get up, boy."

Nick got to his feet slowly. He staggered a little, feeling dizzy with hunger. "I didn't take anything, sir. Honest."

"You talk funny. You're not from here, are you? We got enough problems with the Chinese without snotty runaways roaming the city," the policeman grumbled. "Now turn out your pockets and tell me where you live."

Nick's heart sank. He stuck his hands into his pockets, closing his right hand tightly around the two coins he'd kept safe for so long.

What was it Mr. Hank had said that last day? "Once a picker, always a picker."

A cotton picker. Maybe, after all, the boss man had been right. Maybe that's all he'd ever be.

COTTON PICKER

Before. Before the Lincoln Poor Farm for Indigents and Orphans, there'd been Mr. Hank's farm. Nick and Gran had landed there in late summer, after they'd been driven off their sharecrop.

"I ain't happy about taking in an old lady and a kid," Mr. Hank had grumbled. "But I'm short of hands right about now. If you can keep up and put in a full day's work, you can stay."

"My grandson picks cotton faster than a grown man, Mr. Hank," Gran assured him. "I wouldn't be surprised if he picks a hundred pounds a day when the cotton is at its peak."

Mr. Hank scoffed, "He looks too skinny. Probably lazy, too." And from that moment, Nick made up his mind to try.

For the next two weeks, Nick picked from daybreak to dusk. He came close to bringing in a hundred pounds in a single day, but he never could quite make it.

"Grandson, I'll give you two bits tonight if you can do it," Gran said on that last morning. He bent to give her a sip of tepid water from the dipper.

"We don't have a dime to spare, Gran, never mind a quarter." Nick's heart turned over, but he had to grin. "Not yet, anyhow. But before long, I'll make enough to get us out of here."

"It would sure be nice to have our own house again," she murmured, shaking her head. "I never thought I'd miss that shack on Mr. Greene's place. But where do we go now? No farmer wants to give an old lady and a skinny kid a sharecrop."

"I've got that all worked out, Gran. We're gonna leave Texas and head to California," Nick said all in a rush. He'd been thinking about this plan for so long but had never put it into words before. "I got the idea even before Pa left and we lost the sharecrop. You remember Miss Reedy, my teacher? She told us all about the city of San Francisco. That's where we'll go."

"California? That sounds as far away as the moon." Gran's voice was hoarse, but there was still a twinkle in her warm brown eyes.

"We can get there, Gran, I know it." Nick held her

9

hand in his. He could feel how work had weathered and hardened her skin. "Miss Reedy said San Francisco was the Paris of the Pacific. You know, like Paris, France. It's a great, golden place on a bay of blue water. Tall buildings reach as high as the clouds, and cable cars run up and down hills as steep as cliffs."

Gran shook her head a little. "Now what would we do in a grand place like that?"

"I'll get a job," Nick went on, talking fast, half afraid she'd start laughing and call it a foolish dream. And maybe it was, but now that he'd started, he couldn't stop. "We'll find us a little room. Miss Reedy says there's sometimes a cool fog in San Francisco, so it won't be hot and dusty like here. And we'll never pick cotton again."

"Never pick cotton again . . . ," Gran repeated in a whisper. She looked into Nick's eyes. "Why, I believe I can just see you on the streets of that bright city."

Gran's breath seemed ragged and uneven, as though it hurt to talk. She pressed his hand, then let go. "Now you get on, or Mr. Hank will be mad. And don't fret about me—Elsie Turner promised she'll look in later."

The fields that day had been thick with pickers. Men and women, some as old as Gran. And children, too. Others were so small they could only toddle behind their mamas. Nick knew most everyone by name. Elsie Turner's daughter, Rebecca, had taken to tagging after him.

"Daddy says I can't stop till I fill my bag or I'll get a whipping," she'd whined just the day before. "You pick sooo fast, Nick. Can't you *pleeease* give me some of yours?"

Rebecca asked him this just about every day. As usual, Nick growled in return. "Go away, Rebecca. You can't pick if you're jabbering the whole time."

But that hadn't stopped her questions. "You ever been to school, Nick?"

"Not much," he admitted. "We used to live on a sharecrop before we came here. I'd go to school sometimes, when my pa didn't need me in the fields. I liked parts of it just fine."

"I'm five, too little for school," announced Rebecca. "Did you pick cotton when you were five?"

Nick grunted. "I've picked cotton since I could walk."

On that last morning, Rebecca hadn't bothered him at all. Nick found himself looking around for her. He spotted her in the next row over, her shoulders slumped. Rebecca moved slowly, her small bag trailing behind her. Nick thought a breeze might knock her over.

There had been dew in the early dawn. Nick didn't like picking on dewy mornings. For one thing, it made his clothes damp and cool just when the morning was chill. Worse was what the dampness did to skin.

Nick's fingers were so callused and rough from

picking, he didn't suffer much. But he figured the morning dew had made little Rebecca's skin soft. So soft the hard points of the cotton bolls had dug into her fingers, drawing tiny pricks of blood each time she reached inside to pluck out the white fiber.

"Rebecca," called Nick in a loud hiss. "Scurry up to me and hold open your bag."

In a flash, Nick pulled out an armful of cotton and stuffed it into her sack. Rebecca went back to her row, her bag dragging behind her, too miserable to smile her thanks.

By mid-afternoon, an enormous sun filled a glaring white sky. Nick's sack could have been packed with river rocks, it was that heavy. He wanted to rest, to stretch out between the rows of cotton and fall asleep on the warm earth. Nick felt everything was against him—the sun, the heat, the prickly cotton bolls, the stubborn cotton itself.

I can't give up, Nick told himself. Even if the bag got so heavy it made him weave like a drunken man. Even if the muscles in his shoulders burned into his bones. Sweat stung his eyes, but Nick didn't stop to wipe it away. He made himself keep picking, steady and quick.

Now grab the cotton at its very roots. Now pick it out clean. Right hand, left hand, both together.

A hundred pounds, a hundred pounds, he chanted silently. *A hundred pounds for Gran.*

TOMMY

"You're one of those road kids, ain't you?" The thick-browed policeman kept hold of one of Nick's sleeves and poked at him with his club as if he were checking the tenderness of a piece of meat.

Nick opened his mouth. Nothing came out. He was caught. And then Gran's words came back to him. *I believe I can just see you on the streets of that bright city.*

Nick bent to snatch his cap off the ground. Then he squirmed—hard—wrenching his sleeve out of the policeman's grip.

"Why, you . . ."

Nick willed himself to *move,* feet flying, dodging and ducking through the crowd. He could hear Bushy Brows pounding behind him, panting and wheezing. He sounded madder than a wasp, and he sure didn't seem ready to give up.

"Stop that boy!"

Up ahead, Nick saw two men unloading a large crate from a wagon. They were blocking the sidewalk and seemed to be having trouble getting the crate through a doorway. Nick could hear the men arguing. A small circle had gathered to watch and give advice.

"Turn the crate the other way."

"Put it down first and measure the opening."

The workers backed away from the doorway, calculating their next move. Nick grabbed his chance. Slipping into the circle, he darted between the men and the doorway. He crawled through the legs of the bystanders. And he came out the other side.

Bushy Brows wouldn't catch him now.

Nick slowed to a trot, his breath coming in short gasps. He should duck in somewhere and hide. He couldn't be sure Bushy Brows would give up the chase.

Nick hurried along, head down, not meeting people's eyes. And so at first he didn't notice he'd entered a different neighborhood. It was full of small, busy shops, with bright wooden signs and barrels of food crowding the sidewalks. Even the air had changed, and his nose caught the scent of smoke, fish, and spices.

The streets now were filled mostly with men in simple blue cotton clothes. He walked behind a man who wore a small round hat. His hair was pulled into a long dark braid that hung down his back.

Chinatown. He was in Chinatown. Since he'd arrived in San Francisco a few days ago, Nick had heard people on the street talk about Chinatown, but this was the first time he'd come here.

Nick ducked into a doorway. Next to him, bins displayed fruits and vegetables. Above his head was a large sign with flowing, inky black symbols on it. That, he figured, must be Chinese writing. Nick felt a thrill of excitement. He'd come to the city from Texas. But these people had traveled from the other side of the world.

The world really is big, just like Miss Reedy was always telling us, Nick thought.

15

The writing reminded Nick of Miss Reedy's penmanship lessons—his favorite part of school. Mostly Nick and everyone else in the run-down one-room schoolhouse did lessons in chalk or pencil. Once a week, though, Miss Reedy brought in several real Waterman pens for them to try, along with her prize possession, an old-fashioned glass inkwell decorated with flowing silver leaves. She placed it on the center of her desk, almost like a vase of flowers on a table.

If he closed his eyes, Nick could still see the glass sparkle as that inkwell caught the rays of the morning sun streaming in the window. He'd sure never seen anything like it at home—or anywhere else, for that matter. It was just an ordinary object, a container for ink. But he couldn't help wondering where it had come from. Someone, far away, must have worked hard to make it so beautiful.

All at once the door behind him opened. A Chinese man emerged and nodded. Without thinking, Nick slipped inside. Bushy Brows wouldn't think of looking for him here.

Nick took a few steps and stopped uncertainly. It seemed safe—no one was in sight. He tiptoed behind a shelf toward the back of the store. Maybe he could hide here a little while and then slip out the back into the alley.

Suddenly Nick heard a noise. Sprinting quickly across the wooden floor, he entered a small storeroom in the back. He crouched behind some barrels full of peanuts and held his breath. He didn't think he'd been spotted.

Nick heard voices—a customer must have come in. But Nick couldn't understand a word of the language that was spoken.

Maybe I should run for it, Nick thought. On the other hand, what was the chance of Bushy Brows finding him? Better to stay put.

From his hiding place, Nick peered out at the tiny storeroom, packed with bulky, strange-shaped packages. It was odd—here he was in something that must be a sort of grocery store, yet he had no idea what most of the foods were. Back home they'd always eaten what Gran called the "three M's"—meat, molasses, and meal (short for cornmeal) along with beans and rice. But Nick had no way of knowing what was inside these packages—or how to cook whatever it was.

The sounds stopped. The store grew quiet. Nick rested his head against a barrel. If he hadn't been so nervous, he could almost have fallen asleep.

Crack!

"Ouch. Ow!" Nick yelled, holding his hands over his head. "Stop. Stop hitting me!"

"What are you doing here? Thief!" spat a tall, slim boy.

Nick looked up at a teenage boy, maybe four or five years older than he was. The boy wore a blue, loose-fitting top and pants. Like the men on the street, he had coal black hair gathered tightly into a long braid. With a stern, hard look, he raised the broom handle again.

"Get up." He spat at Nick. "Thief!"

"I . . . I didn't take anything," sputtered Nick, stumbling to his feet. He raised his hands into the air to show they were empty and then quickly put them back to keep the boy from hitting him on the head again.

"Why are you hiding in my store, then?" asked the boy in a cold voice. "You were planning to hit me and rob me. I know your kind."

"No, no, I wasn't," Nick protested. *Think of something to say,* he told himself. *Defend yourself.* But he couldn't. He glanced beyond the boy, measuring the distance to the back door. Maybe he could run for it.

The boy saw his look. He stepped closer, holding the broom against Nick's chest. "You're not running away. I'm going to turn you in to the police."

Nick drew a sharp breath. "No, please. I'll do anything—sweep the store, stock your shelves. The policeman thought I stole something. But I didn't, I swear."

The older boy said nothing. His dark eyes seemed angry.

"I can prove it." Nick reached into his pocket. "If I wanted to buy something, I could. See, I have fifty cents."

18

Nick held his quarters. They were shiny. And no wonder. Nick polished them on his shirt every night. Nick thought about offering the coins to the boy in exchange for safety. But he couldn't. He wouldn't give them up. They were almost all he had to remind him of Gran.

"Just let me stay a little while," Nick added, quickly slipping the coins back into his pocket.

Suddenly Nick wanted to sit down more than anything. His knees felt weak. He licked his dry lips. "Please."

The boy was silent for a long moment, his eyes flicking over Nick's face. Then, to Nick's surprise, he lowered the broom.

"You are new here," he said flatly. "I can tell. The way you talk . . ."

"I come from Texas. I really would work for you. I'm looking for a job," Nick said quickly, hoping the boy wouldn't change his mind and yell for the police. "I . . . I'd take food for pay."

To Nick's surprise, the boy laughed and stood the broom in the corner. "You *are* new. American white boys don't work in Chinatown. They're too busy teasing and tormenting Chinese people."

"Oh." Nick's voice fell. No job, no food.

"I've been teased," Nick offered, trying to think of something to say. "On the county poor farm—an orphanage, really, where I lived this winter. Whenever they took us into town, the kids laughed at us."

The boy shrugged. "Here, even poor kids tease the Chinese. Last week some boys threw stones at me when I was delivering vegetables."

"Are you from China?" Nick was curious. "You, uh, speak good English."

"My parents are from China, but I was born here. I am an American. Though people here don't treat me like one," the boy said in a voice laced with bitterness.

The boy fell silent, as though he thought he had revealed too much. Nick bit his lip, unsure what to say. He looked around at the packages and boxes, all with such strange and beautiful symbols on them. Not like the alphabet at all.

"Can you really understand these squiggly signs?"

"You ask very strange questions for a white boy,"

19

the boy answered, raising his eyebrows. "How could I do business otherwise?"

Nick couldn't imagine being able to read something so different, so extraordinary-looking. He thought again of the crystal-and-silver inkwell on Miss Reedy's desk, which had come from some distant, far-off world. *Chinatown is like a different world, too,* Nick thought. *A different world inside San Francisco itself.*

The tall boy cleared his throat. He seemed to have come to some sort of decision. "Business is slow. It is time for my noon meal of rice and dried fish. Will you join me?"

Nick hesitated.

"No need to pay. I hope you won't mind sitting back here on the floor," the boy added. "I only have one stool. That way you won't be in the way if any customers come in."

Or policemen, thought Nick. For the first time, he looked the boy straight in the eyes and smiled. "Thanks. I'm Nick. Nicholas Dray."

"I have a Chinese name, which you could not pronounce or understand," the boy told him. "But my American name is Tommy. Tommy Liang."

A BOWL OF RICE

Nick tried to use the two sticks Tommy gave him—chopsticks, they were called. But in the end he gave up and ate with his fingers.

"You're very hungry." For the first time, a slight smile crossed Tommy's face as he watched Nick eat.

Nick nodded. The rice was fluffy, white, and hot. Tommy served it in a small, shiny black bowl that felt just right in Nick's hand. "It sure tastes good. You cooked this yourself?"

"I learned to cook after my mother left." Tommy paused with his chopsticks in the air. He spoke matter-of-factly. "She took my younger brothers and sisters back to China. She didn't like America."

"So she just left?" Nick pushed the thought of Pa away.

"It . . . it was too hard for her. I stayed with my

father to help with the store. But then, after he died of pneumonia, my older cousin took over." Tommy looked down at his rice bowl, his face closed. "He is in charge. He goes out with his friends a lot. I do the cooking and look after the store."

Nick wondered if Tommy's cousin was anything like Mr. Hank. "It's a nice store. I'd love to have a shop as fine as this."

Tommy shrugged. "It was my father's dream. But working in a grocery store is not what I hope to do."

Nick was surprised again. "What *do* you want to do?"

Tommy hesitated. "I . . . I love to sing. But becoming a singer is a foolish dream."

Nick looked down at his bowl. He couldn't help thinking of that morning he'd told Gran about *his* dream. They ate in silence until the rice was gone. Tommy filled a small cup with scented, steaming liquid.

"You ate so much. Are you a runaway?" Tommy asked.

Nick nodded. "A few weeks ago, I ran away from the orphanage in Texas."

"Did you live there long?"

"Only a few months. My gran died last fall, in October. My pa is still alive somewhere, I guess." Nick's teacup had no handles. He picked it up gingerly, with two hands, and sipped at the hot liquid. He hoped he wouldn't drop it.

"Up until last summer, Gran, Pa, and I were sharecroppers," he went on. "We worked another man's cotton for a share of the crop. Then, last year, around the end of May, Pa left."

Nick bent his head and felt the warm steam of the tea on his cheek. It had happened just a few weeks after his eleventh birthday. Pa hadn't even tried to explain, Nick remembered. He'd just stuffed a few clothes in a sack and walked out.

"A man can't get ahead sharecropping. Don't blame him. Sharecropping just whittled away at your pa's spirit," Gran had said. "It ain't that he don't love you. He just can't feel one way or another anymore."

"But . . . how could he just leave us here, with . . . this?" Nick had spread out his arms helplessly toward the rows of cotton crowding close to their shack.

Nick couldn't understand how Gran could be so calm, accepting even. True, Gran was Pa's mother-in-law, not his own blood relative. But Pa had walked out on both of them. How could Pa leave his son?

"I'm grateful you're a strong, hardworking boy, Nick," was Gran's only answer. *She's not surprised,* Nick had realized. It was almost as if, all these years, she'd been expecting Pa to leave.

Nick had stared out at the rows of cotton and made himself a promise. "I won't do that. I won't ever walk away."

▐▌▐▌▐▌▐▌

Nick put down his empty teacup and stared at the tiny shreds of tea leaves left at the bottom of the cup. He swallowed hard. He hadn't thought about Pa lately.

"Where did your father go?" Tommy asked. "Is he in San Francisco, too?"

"Pa? Here?" Nick was startled. He tried to imagine what it would be like to see his father's face on a crowded San Francisco street. "Naw. Pa would never leave Texas. I expect when he took off, he hopped a train to Dallas or Austin."

"What happened then?" Tommy asked.

"Not long after Pa left, Mr. Greene ran Gran and me off his farm. Said it was too much for an old woman and kid to run," Nick told him. "After that we got work on a big cotton farm, but I didn't much like Mr. Hank, the boss man there. When Gran passed, he sent me off to an orphanage. The Lincoln Poor Farm for Indigents and Orphans. And then I came here."

Nick rubbed his hands on his pants. It sounded so simple. The whole last year of his life wrapped in a cardboard box of words, he thought. But that's the way he wanted it. He didn't need to open that box and look inside.

Tommy poured Nick more tea. "But why did you choose San Francisco? It is far away from where you lived, isn't it?"

Nick liked how the small teacup fit so nicely in the

palm of his hand. "Gran and I . . . we didn't like cotton anymore. We always planned to come to the city."

Well, that wasn't quite true. But Nick had been telling himself the very same thing every night when he lay on his cot at Lincoln. *Gran wanted to go—she'd want me to take a chance.*

"My parents had a dream of coming here," Tommy said. "But dreams do not always turn out as we hope." Tommy paused and pointed at Nick. "It's easy to see you're a runaway. Your clothes are torn and dirty. How long have you been here?"

Nick counted. "Five nights already."

"And you've been sleeping in alleys and wandering all this time?"

Nick nodded. "It's sure cooler than I thought. And foggy! But I've never seen anything like this place. I love all the tall buildings and that grand hotel—the Palace Hotel. I'd give anything to see the inside of that!

"Market Street is as wide as three roads," Nick went on, his words tumbling out. This boy was the first person he'd really talked to here. "Yesterday I tried to cross it, and all those wagons, cable cars, and shiny black automobiles bumping along the cobblestones like a parade made my head spin."

Tommy shrugged. The city did not impress him.

"You can't wander around like this much longer," Tommy said in a flat voice, placing his cup on a small black tray. "Any policeman who sees you will chase you—and next time you will be caught for sure. They'll put you back in an orphan asylum. I wish I could help, but I can't."

Tommy looked up at the door. Nick scrambled to his feet, his hopes sinking. He hadn't really expected Tommy to help him, but . . .

Tommy let Nick out through the back. "Try to find work in the Produce District or near the piers. And you should sleep south of the Slot."

"The Slot?"

"That's what we call Market Street. Because of the slot in the street for the cable cars. The neighborhoods south of Market are full of immigrants and poor people, so you won't stand out so much."

Nick stopped in front of a sign on the wall. Like the one he'd seen on the street, it was covered with large, flowing symbols. "Those symbols there—they're so strange."

"Not to me," said Tommy. "Those Chinese characters make words and sentences, just like English. And you know, some people are masters at calligraphy, writing characters."

"And . . . and they mean something, right? You said you can understand them?"

"Yes, of course."

Nick waited. "So what does that sign say?"

"That one?" When Tommy smiled, his dark eyes sparkled. "That sign reads: 'Liang's Grocery.'"

ANNIE OF THE NORTH STAR

〽〽〽〽〽

Two mornings later, Nick woke early. He shivered and poked his head out of the doorway. He was in a small alley in the Produce District. It was, he thought, the best place to be. He'd had better luck finding food in garbage cans here than anywhere else.

Nick reached into his pocket, feeling for his quarters. He'd gone so long without spending them, but it was getting harder. Ever since the meal Tommy had given him, his hunger had seemed more painful.

The day before, he'd managed to beg a few hunks of old bread from a bakery and scrounge some rotting fruit from a grocery store. But it wasn't enough.

Sometimes he found himself hitting his stomach, trying to keep it from growling and pinching. The worst part was passing by the open doors of cafés and restaurants and breathing in the good smells of fish or baking bread. He tried not to think about how delicious a bowl of hot soup would taste.

Nick let go of the coins. *Whatever happens, I'm not going to spend them,* he told himself again. He wondered: could he starve in a city full of so many stores, bakeries, hotels, and restaurants? Food was everywhere. But he needed money. And to get money, he needed a job.

Nick rubbed the sleep from his eyes. He was running out of ideas. He'd already begged for work just about everywhere he could think of: grocery stores, a candy store, livery stables, and restaurants. He'd wandered the docks looking for work, too.

Since the day Bushy Brows had chased him into Chinatown, Nick had tried harder to keep a careful lookout. But he knew he couldn't keep it up much longer. Sooner or later, Bushy Brows or one of his fellow officers would get him.

"I can't give up. I have to get a job today." Nick poked his head around a building and scanned the street. He straightened his shoulders and kept his fist in his pocket, closed tight around his quarters. "Today my luck will change. Today I'll find work."

Nick wandered the neighborhoods south of the Slot all morning. It didn't seem to matter where he went or what he said. No one would hire him. Nick caught a glimpse of himself in a window and could see why: he was looking more like a straggly lost dog every day.

In the afternoon, Nick crossed Market Street and headed north up Montgomery, crisscrossing side streets. He went down a pretty cobblestone road called Jackson Street and into a little alley called Balance Street, so short it hardly seemed like a street at all. At the end of the block, he stopped in front of a tall building. " 'The Eiffel Tower Restaurant,' " Nick read.

Paris of the Pacific. That's what Miss Reedy said folks sometimes called San Francisco.

Nick remembered a picture of the real Eiffel Tower in Paris that Miss Reedy had once showed them. Now he recognized the shape of the famous tower on the sign before him. Nick sniffed. The air here seemed scented with spices and coffee. It might not be Paris, but it seemed as far away from the cotton fields as Nick had ever imagined he could be.

I'm really here, Nick thought, forgetting for a moment his hunger and need for work. Suddenly he longed for Gran so hard it hurt. How amazed she would have been at all the tall buildings and smart-looking people and the boats tooting in the bay.

Nick spotted a lodging house, a butcher, a couple of grocery stores, and a wine company. On Jackson Street and Jones Alley was a large building called A. P. Hotaling and Co., which advertised "Old Kirk Whiskey."

29

Nick stopped in front of another store a few doors away, "Columbia Coffee & Spice Company." That must be why he could smell those spicy scents.

These were stores he had never imagined, selling items he'd never tasted or seen. A well-dressed man passed by. Nick pictured himself as a businessman one day. Why, he might even have to go to Paris to buy wine or spices. He could see the real Eiffel Tower.

Nick was still daydreaming when he caught sight of it, nestled in a row of low buildings near the corner of Balance and Jackson streets. Nick walked over and pressed his nose against the large plate glass window. He brought his hands up to shade his eyes against the glare.

"Wow," breathed Nick. "Look at that."

Paper. This store was filled with paper. Nick could see stacks of large journals bound in dark, rich leather. A display of shiny new pens, laid out on forest green velvet, filled the window. Near the pens sat several gleaming glass inkwells, their delicate silver leaves and flowers shining like mirrors.

"Wow . . . ," Nick said again. He wondered if this was the store where Miss Reedy got her pens and inkwell when she'd come to the city.

Nick stared at the silver leaves. Something tugged at his memory. That spring when he and Gran had found some wild daisies in the field. They'd dug them up and planted them in an old tin can.

"Oh, I do love wild daisies," Gran had said, her eyes sparkling. "Your mother and I used to pick them when she was your age. She liked to pluck off the petals, one by one. Well, I suppose most children do that. We'll keep these ones nice right here in front. The sun will sparkle on the tin can like silver."

Silver. Just like the silver leaves on the inkwell, the flowers in the old tin can seemed to promise something. But the flowers hadn't lasted. The daisies had shriveled in the baking sun. The dirt in the can turned hard and cracked. One night, when Nick and Pa had straggled home late from the fields, Pa had reached down, seized the old can, and flung it away with all his might.

31

Nick stepped back to read the sign on the door: PAT PATTERSON, STATIONER.

Nick noticed something else. The store was closed and there was a handwritten note.

He read it aloud. "'Out on delivery. Will return shortly. Please be patient and look at the sky or sing. The wait will be worth it!'"

Nick found himself grinning. He stood in front of the store for ten full minutes. Then he began to pace. A new idea had come into his head, and he turned it over this way and that, trying to find the courage to carry it out.

Nick walked to the corner of Jackson and Montgomery, then back again. He walked in the other direction, to Sansome Street, where he could see a large, official-looking building, with clerks and businessmen streaming in and out.

He crossed Sansome and headed back toward the store, up a narrow alleyway called Gold Street. Gold Street. Gold had been discovered years ago in California, he knew. This seemed to be a good sign. Maybe his luck would change.

Nick kept a careful watch for police officers. He didn't want to get chased away by someone like Bushy Brows. No, not yet. Not until he tried out his crazy idea. Back on Jackson, Nick was disappointed to find that the stationer's store was still closed. Where was Mr. Pat Patterson? Nick wondered.

32

A sandy-haired girl about eight years old came out of a store and passed close by, carrying a small packet. Then she turned, stopped in front of Nick, and planted her feet.

"Hullo. I saw you standing here a few minutes ago. And now you're back. Do you live here? Are you moving into the rooming house on the corner there?" she demanded, pointing toward Montgomery Street. "That's where my mama and I live."

Nick shifted his feet and shook his head without speaking. Something about this girl made him feel off balance. It took him a minute to realize what it was: one of her eyes was a hazel brown, the other a pale gray-blue. She wore her hair in braids. Her plain blue dress was threadbare but clean.

"That's too bad." The girl with the strange eyes made no move to leave. "I'd like it if you did. It's mostly grown-ups and old sailors in there now. At night the old man in the apartment next to ours coughs and spits."

She demonstrated, making a loud, coughing sound. Then, expertly, she spat on the ground.

"My grandmother said girls shouldn't spit," Nick told her. "Why don't you go home now?"

He wished she'd go away. He'd made up his mind to talk to the owner of the stationer's store—this Mr. Patterson. And he had to go over in his head what to say. Nick didn't want to take the chance of this girl ruining his plan with her chatter or awful spitting.

The girl didn't seem to hear his question.

"If you did move in, we could play together. I've always wanted a big brother to talk to," she said brightly. "Of course, you'd just be a friend. Because once you're the oldest, you usually can't get a big brother. My mother wishes I had a big sister, someone to show me how to be a lady. She says I talk a lot—too much for a girl."

"Maybe she's—" Nick began.

But the girl had only stopped to catch her breath. "I don't have any brothers or sisters at all, so I have to talk to people I meet." She bounced from one foot to the other, then leaned forward as if to tell him a secret. "Everything is going to change, though. Soon I will be a big sister."

33

"Won't your mother need that parcel you just bought?" Nick tried again. He could imagine why this girl's mother sent her on errands.

"Oh, no. She's taking a nap. She said very clearly, 'Please don't bother me for thirty minutes.' And that was only about twenty minutes ago, I think," the girl went on, hopping up and down again, first on one foot, then the other. "I have a lot of energy. I'm exactly eight now, and of course I never take naps. Even when I was little, I didn't. But when a woman is about to have a baby, she has to take lots of naps. Did you know that?"

"Uh, no, I didn't." Nick glanced down the street. He wished the owner would come soon.

"I like talking to you. My name is Annie. Annie Sheridan," she told him. Not only were her eyes different colors, Nick realized, but they bulged out a little, like a fish's. Her face was so much eyes it was hard to notice anything else—except her chatter.

"That's a nice name," said Nick automatically. He wondered what was in her parcel. Could it be food? Maybe she would have a kind heart. He wondered if he should ask her for something to eat.

"My daddy is gone on a boat, but he's coming back," Annie went on, rocking from one foot to the other. She stuck her nose in the air and threw back her shoulders. "I'm in charge until then, especially when I'm not in school. I really am. I have to look after Mama. Do you believe me?"

34

"Sure, I believe you," said Nick. "Where did your father go?"

"Out to sea somewhere—I don't know for sure." Annie waved her hand vaguely in the direction of the bay. "The sea is very large. It's scary to think about a little boat on a big, big sea. Sometimes I lie awake at night and fly to the North Star so I can look down at my daddy's boat and help him find his way."

Despite himself, Nick couldn't help grinning. Something about her persistence seemed familiar. "So, Annie of the North Star, does that work?"

"I won't know, will I? Not until Daddy comes back," she said a little crossly. "But I'm sure he will. He promised. He says it's important not to give up believing in people. Sometimes believing is what makes things happen."

People disappear all the time and don't come back, Nick wanted to tell her. But he didn't. She seemed so certain.

Of course, considered Nick, she might be making it all up. It might just be a story she told herself at night. The girl's father might not be at sea at all. It was more likely that he'd taken off, like Pa had, leaving Annie and her mother to fend for themselves in the city.

Annie frowned and looked at him. She pointed at the hole in his pant leg. "You talk funny. You look poor and dirty. I bet you don't have many friends. I suppose

I could be your friend, even if you don't live in my rooming house. What's your name?"

Nick was getting anxious. He wanted to be standing alone in front of the beautiful stationery store when the owner arrived. He had to get free of this persistent girl.

"I don't need any friends. I just need a job," he said quickly. It wasn't hard to be mean; he'd gotten good at it at Lincoln. He hadn't let anyone be friends with him then. He'd never admitted to being an orphan like the rest of them.

Nick took a breath. "Go home now, will you? You're bothering me."

Annie flashed him a look, her large, strange eyes wide with hurt. Then, shoulders slumping, she walked slowly down the street in the direction of the rooming house.

Looking after her, Nick was suddenly reminded of little Rebecca, picking cotton in the fields with her small shoulders bent against the pain.

He sighed and called out, "Hey, Annie. My name's Nick. Good luck being a big sister."

Annie turned sharply. She waved, her face lit with a big smile. Then she skipped toward home, hopping from one cobblestone to another.

This little girl really *was* like Rebecca. Nick reached into his pocket to touch one of his coins. He wondered where Rebecca was now. Probably still on Mr. Hank's place as a migrant field hand or some other farm like it. After all, it was April again, planting season. Nick swallowed. Spring. His first spring without Gran.

"Well, I may be a road kid, but I'm not in the fields anymore, Gran," Nick whispered. It was the first time since before he could remember when he wasn't planting cotton seed. Planting first. Then came thinning the young seedlings and chopping to keep weeds away. And then in the fall came the harvest, the picking.

It was funny. Up to now, everything—what he ate, how much food they had, even whether he went to school or not—was tied to cotton. But here in the city, most folks probably didn't even know what a cotton plant looked like or what it felt like in your hands. Why, most likely they bought their clothes ready-made from a store without even thinking where the cloth came from.

I could go back, Nick thought. *If I can't find a job here after all, if Bushy Brows or some other policeman catches me, I could go to an orphanage or some poor farm. Or I could go back to the fields on my own.*

He was good at picking cotton. He could earn his own living. Living in tents with other migrant workers, maybe working his way back up to a sharecrop . . .

Nick looked down at his hands, callused from field work. Hours and hours, days and days. Hot, flat fields.

No. Nick shook his head. No matter what, he didn't want to look up into the same empty wide sky again.

37

Here the sky wasn't empty. It was broken by tall buildings that rose high into the air. The newspaper building—the Call Building, people called it—must be two or three hundred feet high, Nick thought. You glimpsed the sky and the sun between the buildings, but the sun didn't press down on you. People had made this city. It was lively and noisy and full.

Whatever happened, he didn't want to go back to the fields.

PARIS OF THE PACIFIC

Just when Nick was ready to give up waiting in front of the stationery store, a man turned the corner. He strode jauntily down the street, wearing a sharp gray suit, a round derby hat, and shiny black shoes. He was whistling merrily, tipping his hat at people he passed. By his side trotted the most beautiful golden dog Nick had ever seen.

As the pair strode by, Nick couldn't help smiling. The man threw a quick, quizzical glance at him, raising his eyebrows into little sideways question marks. Then, still whistling, he stopped in front of the stationery store. He drew out a key from his pocket with a flourish and put it in the lock in one quick motion.

Nick didn't move. He kept smiling. He could feel his palms getting sweaty.

The man stopped whistling and turned around. "Hullo. Scat, kid! I'm sorry, but I've nothing to eat.

This isn't a grocery or a charity kitchen, you know. We sell paper and pens, not pumpkins and porridge."

Nick flushed. At that moment the golden dog trotted over and planted himself on Nick's shoes. His feathery tail whisked back and forth on the sidewalk with a soft, swishing sound. The dog stared up at Nick with friendly brown eyes. He whined a little, deep in his throat. Then he opened his mouth and smiled right at Nick.

Nick grinned and scratched the dog's head. "I think he likes me."

"Humph," said the dog's owner.

Nick looked more closely at the man. He had dark brown eyes, set wide apart. They gave him a surprised look even when his eyebrows weren't raised. *Maybe that's why he whistles,* Nick thought. *He looks like someone who has a hard time being serious.*

The man swung the door open. "Nice try, but I'm not impressed. This dog likes everyone, don't you, Shake? And why not? You're the friendliest dog in San Francisco. I believe you'd trot home with every customer if I let you. Come on."

Nick moved forward.

"Not you. I was speaking to Shake here. As I explained just seconds ago, I don't have any food for beggars."

Nick took a breath. "Don't give me food. Give me a job."

"A job? Good heavens. What kind of a job? I don't need a helper!" The man seemed genuinely startled.

Nick could feel his heart beating hard. "But you do."

The man's mouth fell open. His eyes grew wider than ever. "I do?"

"Yes, sir. You do. You need me, sir. I've been standing here for at least fifteen minutes, waiting." Nick spoke quickly, the words tumbling out. "Why, suppose I was a rich gentleman in need of a new pen or a journal for my business. Or a clerk from that big building down over on Sansome Street. Or what if I was a lady who wanted a beautiful inkwell? What then?"

"What then?" the man repeated, striding across the floor to the counter.

"Well, you'd have lost a customer then, wouldn't you?" Nick said, stepping through the doorway. He took off his hat and felt his hair spill out onto his forehead. "Please, sir. Why don't you try me out for just a few days? I'm a hard worker. I can sweep and clean up. I can do the deliveries while you make important sales."

Nick crumpled his cap in his hands. He wasn't sure if the man was even listening, but at least he hadn't thrown him out—yet.

"I like drawing and paper and writing. My penmanship is good. Real good. Even Miss Reedy said so, back in Texas. She had an inkwell, too, like those shiny ones

41

in your window. Maybe I could help demonstrate your pens and your ink." Nick searched his mind for something, anything, to say. "Why, I'd even like to learn how to write fancy. What is it called? Oh, calli . . . calli . . ."

"Calligraphy?" suggested the man, a slight grin turning the corner of one side of his mouth.

"Yes, that's it. Calli . . . calligraphy." Nick stumbled over the unfamiliar word. "It's that beautiful, fancy writing, like art, like what the Chinese people do with their . . . designs."

At last, Nick ran out of breath. The man walked over and stared down at him. Nick couldn't read the expression on his face.

"Characters."

"Pardon me, sir?"

"They are called characters, not designs. Chinese characters."

The man went to a table in the corner, took out a journal, and began to make some notes. Nick stood quietly, waiting, trying not to breathe too loudly.

"Quite a salesman, aren't you?" the man said after a moment. "What are you, kid, about ten years old?"

Nick drew himself up taller. "I'll be twelve this month—April twenty-third."

"Hmmm . . . Today's Monday, the sixteenth. That's next week. I'd say you don't have a very pleasant birthday coming up. No, it's not my idea of how to spend a

42

birthday at all, sleeping in an alley and so forth. Which, I gather from the look and smell of you, is what you have been doing."

The man put down his pen, turned around, and folded his arms. He leaned back against the table, crossing his shiny shoes, and considered Nick. "Run away from home? South of the Slot somewhere?"

"I didn't run away from home, exactly. I . . . I came from the fields," Nick sputtered. He supposed a county poor farm was the fields.

"You came from the fields?" Mr. Pat Patterson turned toward his dog. "Did you hear that, boy? He came from the fields!"

Nick tried again. "From a county poor farm in Texas. An orphanage, really. I was sent there after I lost my gran. But I've wanted to come here for a long time. So I ran away."

"Why here?" Mr. Pat Patterson spread his hands wide.

"I just . . . I had a feeling about it. Like the city was a bright light that I needed to get to . . . Like I belong here."

When he tried to put it into words, it sounded silly. But Nick went on anyway. "I want to live in San Francisco because it's the Paris of the Pacific."

The man threw his head back and laughed out loud, a bright sharp guffaw, his brown eyes twinkling. Shake

43

barked along with him, a wide grin lighting his face. "So, you came from the fields to live here, in the Paris of the Pacific. Let me ask you, then: how *do* we know where we belong?"

Nick stared at the floor, his mind a blank. No one had ever asked him such a question. At first he couldn't imagine that the man actually expected an answer. But when he looked up, Mr. Pat Patterson was still staring at him, eyebrows raised.

"Well, sir. I think maybe people are like plants, at least a little." Nick struggled to find the words. "Different plants need different places. Like cotton. Cotton needs warm weather. It wouldn't grow in a chilly, foggy place like San Francisco. Today, this morning, anyway, it's been nice. But there've been some days when a cold, chill mist seems to settle over everything."

Nick shivered a little, thinking about how hard it had been to get warm on those mornings. "Cotton wouldn't like that kind of weather at all. It wouldn't grow. So, maybe . . . maybe people are like that, too. Some places just fit us better than others."

Mr. Pat Patterson didn't laugh this time. He looked Nick up and down. "At this moment, it doesn't appear that this glittering city where you think you belong is treating you so well. We're right near Gold Street, you know," he went on. "Lots of people have come here looking for gold. But they haven't always found it."

Nick shifted his feet and looked down at his hands.

44

They were dirty, with dark ridges under his fingernails. He should have tried to clean himself up better. This wasn't going to work. Mr. Pat Patterson was toying with him, like a cat with a field mouse. Nick twisted his hat hard.

"Have you ever worked, young fellow?"

"Yes, sir, I've worked." Nick looked up then. He squared his shoulders and looked straight into the man's eyes. His voice was firm. "I've worked since I could walk. Once—once I even picked a hundred and seven pounds of cotton in a single day."

A Hundred Pounds
꽃꽃꽃꽃꽃

That bag of cotton had been the heaviest one Nick had ever dragged behind him. By sundown on that last day, when folks started weighing up, Nick felt sure he'd have good news to bring to Gran.

Mr. Hank, the boss, had been waiting by the wagon where the weigher was hooked up. Mr. Hank was a thin rail of a man with a sharp voice. His eyes were small and close together. Sometimes Mr. Hank stared at Nick so hard he felt guilty, even if he hadn't done anything wrong.

Nick had hung back, wanting to pick the last row clean. *This bag is so heavy it's just got to be a hundred pounds,* he thought.

"Come on, kid. I ain't got all night," Mr. Hank bellowed.

Nick made his way awkwardly to the wagon, his

breath coming in short pants. Usually a few people slumped nearby or sat on the ground, hoping Mr. Hank would give them a ride back to camp.

That night the crowd seemed larger than usual. Ten or twelve people stood solemnly together. They stared at Nick, almost as if they'd been waiting for him to finish.

Nick wondered how they knew this was an important weighing for him.

He imagined folks bursting into applause. *See that skinny boy with the curly hair?* they'd say. *You'd never know it to look at him, but he sure can pick!*

Nick spotted Rebecca, leaning against her mother. Elsie Turner was a bony, rough-faced woman in a faded blue dress. Her look was hard, but she'd been real kind to Gran. Rebecca pointed at Nick, tugged at her mother's skirt, and whispered something her mother bent to hear.

"You sure took your time. You been slacking off to-day, kid?" Mr. Hank grumbled, reaching out for Nick's sack.

Mr. Hank, Nick thought, was the kind who could watch you pick from morning till night and still suspect you of weighing down your sack with stones or wet cotton to make it heavier.

"No, sir," said Nick, slipping the strap of the bag off his right shoulder. "Picked steady. I want to show my grandmother I can pick a hundred pounds."

47

"You're the Dray kid," Mr. Hank said then, lifting Nick's bag onto the weighing hook.

"Yes, sir. Nick Dray."

Mr. Hank nodded to a stocky, red-faced man Nick hadn't noticed before. The man stepped forward, a wan smile pasted on his lips.

Nick wondered what the man was doing there. He seemed out of place. He wasn't dressed for field work, for one thing. He wore dark pants and suspenders, with his belly bulging through the buttons of his shirt. Sweat poured down the sides of his brown hat. The man pulled out a white handkerchief, shook it, and then wiped his forehead.

Mr. Hank nodded again to the stranger. "This is the one, Jim. I ain't going to be responsible. You go with Mr. Kelly here, Nick. He'll bring you to the county poor farm where you belong. They can take orphans there."

Nick stared blankly at the man. County poor farm! Orphans!

Mr. Kelly put his handkerchief in his pocket. He grabbed Nick's elbow. "Come along, son. You're done here."

At first Nick didn't take it in—and then he didn't want to. *Something awful has happened to Gran. Mr. Kelly is here for me.*

Nick pulled his arm away hard and turned to

48

the boss. "The cotton. How much? How much cotton did I pick?" It was hard to get the words out. "Gran said she'd give me two bits if I picked a hundred pounds."

Mr. Hank stepped back and squinted at the numbers on the scale. "Hmmm . . . hundred and seven pounds. I'll deduct your pay from what your grandmother owed me. I lost money on you folks, I hope you know."

Nick's head felt light. He took a step back from the men.

Mr. Kelly cleared his throat and reached out a puffy hand to grab Nick's elbow. Nick shook him off and looked at Rebecca's mother. "Gran had a fever, that's all. She's strong."

I should have done more. It's my fault. I should have known. Suddenly Nick felt like he couldn't breathe. He'd made a terrible mistake. So terrible he couldn't bear it. He'd thought all he had to do was pick a hundred pounds of cotton to make Gran feel better, to cheer her up. But that wasn't any help at all. It wasn't what she had needed.

"She *was* strong, boy," said Mrs. Turner, moving her hand wearily to push a wisp of thin hair from her eyes. "But this afternoon, her heart just gave out. It was her time. You couldn't have known. She's earned her rest."

Nick shook his head. He wanted to protest, to scream: *I shoulda done more, tried to get a doctor, get her help, get her away.*

Mrs. Turner put something in Rebecca's hand. "Go on, honey."

Rebecca walked slowly across the open space. She stuck out her arm. It was sunburned and scratched. "Here's fifty cents. Two quarters. One's from your gran. She gave it to Ma this afternoon before she passed and said it was for you. The other is from us."

Rebecca panted a little. It was probably the longest speech of her life.

Nick held out his hand, and Rebecca dropped the two coins into it. She stared at them for a minute and sighed. It was a lot of money to her. Rebecca turned to look back at her mother, who nodded her on. "Go on, honey, say the rest of it to the boy."

"Ma says to say you were a good grandson. And we're very, very sorry for your loss," Rebecca blurted. She ran back and hid her face in her mother's dress.

Nick closed his fist tight around the coins. He turned to Mr. Hank, who was busy adding up numbers. Adding his profits for the day. Gran's death meant nothing to him. The boss hadn't called Nick out of the field. Didn't want to lose a day of picking, most likely.

"Last row!" Nick spat. "That's the last row of cotton I'll ever pick, mister."

Mr. Hank snorted, then laughed. "Last row? I don't think so. What else you gonna do? Can't start a fire with wet kindling, kid. Once a picker, always a picker."

One Chance

𝍢𝍢𝍢𝍢𝍢𝍢

"What did you say your name was, young man?" Pat Patterson asked.

They were sitting in chairs at the back of the store. Afterward, Nick was never sure exactly what caused Pat Patterson to change his mind. Maybe it was that Nick just kept standing there. Or maybe it was the moment that, with a big sigh, the large golden dog had stretched out on his back across Nick's feet, begging to have his belly scratched.

"All right, Shake, my boy, I get the point." Mr. Pat Patterson threw his hands up in the air with a sigh. "Let's all have some nourishment, shall we? Just the thought of toiling all day in the blazing sun has made me parched and ravenous."

After rummaging in a cupboard, Mr. Pat Patterson brought out two bottles of warm root beer and some generous slices of bread with cheese. The dog jumped up and stationed himself nearby, his plumy tail wagging like a pendulum.

Nick swallowed. "I didn't say what my name was, sir. It's Nick. Nicholas Dray, sir."

"All right, Nicholas," mumbled the stationer, his mouth full. "Just because I'm feeding you, don't get the wrong idea."

"I'll try not to, sir."

"And for God's sake, don't call me sir. Call me Pat. Everyone in San Francisco does. Except Shake here. He just barks. Isn't that right, boy?" Pat broke off a piece of bread and tossed it to the dog.

The dog snatched it out of the air with a quick snap, sat back on his haunches, and barked for more, his white teeth gleaming in a happy smile. He stood in front of Nick, tail wagging hard.

Nick reached out to rub Shake's black velvet nose. "When he wags his tail, his whole body wiggles and shakes, too. Especially, you know, the back part. I guess that must be why you named him Shake, isn't it?"

Mr. Pat chortled. "Well, I must say I never thought of it quite that way. As a matter of fact, Shake is short for Shakespeare. He's named after the bard himself— William Shakespeare."

Nick felt his face getting red. William Shakespeare. He tried to remember what Miss Reedy had told them about William Shakespeare. About all Nick could remember was that Shakespeare lived a long time ago in

England. Nick thought maybe he'd written plays. Yes, that was it. But he hoped Mr. Pat wouldn't start asking him too many questions about any of them.

Why couldn't Mr. Pat have named his dog something simple, like King or Brownie? Nick shook his head. He tried to focus on what Mr. Pat Patterson was saying.

Mr. Pat was waving a gleaming silver pen in Nick's direction. He stood up straight, as if he were about to make a speech. Maybe Mr. Pat was an actor. That might explain why he'd given his dog such a funny name.

"Let me say at the outset, right from the top, Nicholas, that I am not the fatherly type. I don't want a son. Shakespeare's the only family I've got."

"Yes, Mr. Pat."

"So, the best advice I can give you is to go turn yourself in at the nearest orphanage—"

"But—" put in Nick.

"Hear me out. That's the *best* advice I can give you. But clearly you are loath to take it," Mr. Pat declared firmly with a shake of his pen. "No, you seem to have a spirit of independence and a sense of courage. And, I might add, an appreciation for writing and letters that is somewhat surprising in one of your background."

Mr. Pat waved his hands proudly toward his store. Nick could barely follow what the man said from one moment to the next.

54

"I myself am a writer, you know," Mr. Pat went on. "Not on the level of the beloved bard, of course."

"You mean Shakespeare?" Nick asked.

The dog barked. His master nodded. "Exactly. Or even a fresh American talent like Jack London. Have you read his *Call of the Wild*? Magnificent."

Mr. Pat scratched his nose with one long finger. "Let's see, it came out, when was it? Three years ago, I think. Yes, that's right, because that's when I got Shakespeare here. He's barely over his puppyhood! I almost named him Buck, after the dog in London's book. But Shakespeare seemed a better fit with the stationery business, wouldn't you agree?"

As if he knew he was being talked about, Shakespeare sat back on his haunches with a broad grin, his bright chocolate brown eyes darting from Nick to his master. Then he padded over to Nick and put his head in Nick's lap.

"What a glutton for scratches that dog is," remarked Mr. Pat. "He does seem to have really taken to you, young man."

Nick grinned. "Do you think so? I never saw a dog with such sparkly brown eyes before. When he opens his mouth, he smiles like a person." Nick loved the way Shake's soft fur felt under his hand.

"Now, then, what was I saying?"

"That you're a writer?" Nick offered.

"Ah, yes, that was it. Indeed I am. Well, not actually

in print, like those luminaries who live on the other side of Montgomery Block."

"Montgomery Block?"

Mr. Pat swept his hands wide. "It's our little corner of San Francisco. That big block of a building at the end of the street is the U.S. Customs House—also called the Appraisers' Building. Across from us is Hotaling's whiskey, where my esteemed friend Ed Lind toils away on the accounts like a veritable Bob Cratchet. (Forgive me, Nicholas, that's a reference to Dickens.) We have wine merchants, a rooming house, and a coffee-and-spice store. And where Montgomery hits Washington is a building where many writers live."

Nick's head was whirling. "It all just looks like buildings to me, sir."

"A city is always more than its buildings. Buildings, of course, have their own characters. But I find that the true heart of a city is its people, always so fascinating and different. That's what I love about San Francisco, don't you?"

"I . . . I haven't actually met any fascinating people yet," Nick said. He almost added, "Except you."

"Well, you will. At any rate, I think you can see why my little store is so perfectly situated here on Jackson Street. And although my literary hopes may never come to fruition, we haven't been doing too badly in business, have we, faithful canine companion?"

Shakespeare jerked his head up and gave two sharp barks, baring his white teeth in a bright grin of agreement. *It's almost as if they're real friends who understand each other,* Nick thought. He gripped the hat Gran had bought for him and looked up, wishing he could say something to make Mr. Pat like him.

"I think your store is amazing, sir. Especially the inkwells and the pens, too. I wonder . . . I wonder if my teacher Miss Reedy bought her beautiful inkwell right here." Nick gestured toward the gleaming glass cases in the front window.

"And maybe she ate in that Eiffel Tower Restaurant I saw just down the street. It sure was a pretty inkwell. Well, more than pretty." Nick let out a breath. This wasn't working. He didn't know how to talk to a city person.

But Mr. Pat was nodding. "Yes, indeed, Nicholas. Aim for precision in language at all times. These inkwells *are* more than just pretty. They are exquisite, luminous, superb. But don't get me started. I may have to show you my collection of old and rare inkwells, mostly from France and England.

"So, it certainly seems clear that, unschooled as you are, you have an appreciation, a nose, we might say," Mr. Pat continued, leaning forward and tapping his own pointed nose with the tip of the silver pen, "for the finer things.

57

"But! And I must warn you this is an important 'but'—our relationship must entirely be one of employer and employee," he warned. "I expect absolute integrity and honesty. Absolute honesty! That is what I get from Shakespeare, after all. So, let us enter into a contract. You have one chance to prove yourself. One chance only. Do we understand each other, young Nicholas?"

"I . . . I think so. I guess. . . ." Nick stopped. He wasn't sure he understood anything. He gulped, his heart beating fast, almost afraid to ask the question. "Does this mean that you're . . . you're giving me a job?"

Nick's job, as it turned out, was to watch the store for two days.

"This week I have some business in Oakland, across the bay. Just a couple of days," Pat Patterson explained. "Unfortunately, I must leave Tuesday evening."

"Unfortunately?" Nick asked, scratching behind Shakespeare's ear. The big dog leaned against him and sighed. Nick was starting to get used to Mr. Pat's unexpected way of talking. Not that Nick actually *understood* everything Mr. Pat said, but at least he didn't feel quite so nervous.

"Don't you know? Oh, well, now, that's right. How could you? I said it was unfortunate, Nicholas, because being gone Tuesday evening means I'll miss the rare and wonderful opportunity to hear Enrico Caruso sing the role of Don Jose in *Carmen* at the Grand Opera House. But business calls, and it can't be helped."

Nick's face must have betrayed his confusion. Mr. Pat laughed. "Ah, you don't know who Caruso is, do you?"

Nick shook his head and felt his face flush. "Or . . . or Don whatever, either."

"Now, Nicholas, another rule of the establishment. Never be afraid to ask questions," Mr. Pat proclaimed, pointing a thin finger at Nick. "It is not your fault that you've never heard of Caruso. But it will be if you choose to remain in ignorance."

Nick looked down at his feet. He did feel stupid and ignorant most of the time. Especially now. About the only thing he knew was cotton. *Well, at least I know more about that than Mr. Pat.*

Nick thought back to all the school days he and the other sharecropper kids had missed so they could work in the fields. Usually, from about late September until November, the whole school would close. Nick hadn't given it much thought at the time. After all, cotton came first. It always had.

"Anyway, Nicholas, I won't be gone long. I should be back late Thursday afternoon," Mr. Pat was saying.

Nick looked around the shop, panic in his voice. "If you're leaving tomorrow night, I . . . I don't think I can learn all the prices by then."

"Good heavens, boy. Do you take me for a fool? I have no intention of leaving you in charge of working in my shop. No, the shop will be closed and locked." Mr. Pat's voice was firm.

"Then what will my job be?"

"To keep watch over the shop and take care of Shakespeare, of course. You can stay in the basement with our noble canine companion here." Mr. Pat bowed toward his dog. "I have an office down there with my important papers—business records and so forth. There's a little sitting room outside the office that should suit you. There's only one small window, but it's comfortable enough."

60

He nodded, apparently quite satisfied with his plan. "Yes, this should work out quite well. I was a bit nervous about leaving and taking Shakespeare with me, as I had a robbery last month. So if you see anyone suspicious loitering around, run for a police officer."

"A police officer?" Nick swallowed hard. He wasn't sure how he felt about running *toward* a policeman.

"Oh, there's usually one or two to be found on Market Street. Mind you, some of them can't run all that fast."

Nick couldn't help smiling to himself as he pictured Bushy Brows lumbering after him.

"Now, Nick, may I have your promise that when I return, Shakespeare here will be happy and well fed?"

"Oh, yes, sir."

"And that none of my papers or the treasures we store here will be disturbed?"

Nick nodded.

"Excellent. If my business deal goes well, perhaps we'll stroll over to the old Eiffel Tower Restaurant on Thursday evening and pretend we're in Paris."

Nick felt a smile grow at the corners of his mouth and spread across his face. He had a job and a roof over his head. He might even eat in a restaurant.

Suddenly Nick felt light and free. He imagined this was how a small cloud must feel skittering across a clear sky.

Nick rested his hand on Shakespeare's head. "I don't need to pretend I'm in Paris, Mr. Pat. Just being here in San Francisco is fine with me."

Something Unexpected & Unseen

On Tuesday evening, Nick stood on Jackson Street with his hand around Shake's collar.

"Better hold him, Nicholas," Mr. Pat counseled. "He's a faithful companion and likes to follow me. But if he should stray, don't worry too much. Shakespeare can find his way home from anywhere in the city."

Nick watched Mr. Pat Patterson stroll down the street and turn the corner at Sansome. Mr. Pat turned and waved cheerfully. "Until Thursday, then. Keep safe and strong."

Nick waved back and Shakespeare whined a little, pulling at his collar. "No, you're staying with me this time, boy."

There was a part of Nick that wished he could go with Mr. Pat, too. It would be lonely without him. And then there was the responsibility of the store. Nick's stomach felt fluttery. Not empty, thanks to Mr. Pat's generosity, but nervous.

Things had changed so suddenly. He was no longer Nicholas Dray, cotton picker. Or Nick the Invisible, road kid. No, he was now in charge of what was, so far as he could tell, the most beautiful store in San Francisco. True, the store was closed and locked up safe, but that didn't matter. It was a big job.

Nick cleared his throat. "Come on, Shakespeare. Let's go downstairs and keep watch."

He felt a tap on his shoulder. He whirled around just as Annie Sheridan jumped out in front of him, hopping up and down on the cobblestones, her braids bouncing in the air.

"I heard! I heard everything he said," she chortled.

Nick frowned. "Where did you come from? Were you spying on me?"

She pouted. "I couldn't help hearing. I was just coming out of the alley. Besides, I already guessed. I saw you, Mr. Pat, and Shakespeare on your way to the store this morning."

"So you know Mr. Pat?"

"Everyone knows Mr. Pat. He's very funny." Annie paused for breath and waved to a tall young man entering a building on the corner of Jones Alley and Jackson Street. "Oh, and there's Mr. Lind! Hello!" she called out.

"Hullo there yourself, Annie. Who's your young

friend?" Nick was surprised to see the man stroll over and greet Annie with a little bow.

"This is Nick, Mr. Lind. He's new. Mr. Pat has hired him, and he's going to live here forever and be my friend," Annie explained importantly. "Nick, this is Mr. Ed Lind. He works *a lot*. He hardly ever has time to talk on account of he's practically in charge of Hotaling's there. That's the whiskey warehouse—and it's the best whiskey in California!"

"Thanks for the compliment, young miss. But I hope you haven't tried our whiskey yourself," Mr. Lind teased.

"Of course not! Sometimes the men in the rooming house come home at night smelling of whiskey. It's awful." Annie scrunched up her nose.

"Well, I'd better get back to work." Mr. Lind tipped his hat. "Nice to meet you, Nick. You'll enjoy working for Pat. He and that dog of his really light up this street."

Annie watched Ed Lind walk back to the warehouse. She twirled one of her braids around her fingers thoughtfully. "I think it's important to have a lot of friends in our neighborhood. It's almost like having a bigger family. Mama says making friends is my special gift. What's yours, Nick?"

"Mine?"

Annie stared up at him with her bright, mismatched eyes. "Your special gift. Something you do better than anything."

64

"I don't know, Annie," Nick lied.

"Well, I'm sure you'll think of something," Annie went on, barely pausing for his answer. "Hey, I know something. You're good at shopping. I see you have a new set of clothes. And I bet I know how you got them, too. Mr. Pat! Did he take you to the Emporium?"

Nick nodded. Mr. Pat had marched him into the huge department store on Market Street. Nick's jaw had dropped in amazement at the sparkling lights and displays. Mr. Pat had finally reminded him to close his mouth.

"I've never had ready-made pants and shirts before," Nick told Annie.

He had to admit it was nice to have someone to talk to. Of course, it would be a lot better if he had a real friend his own age to talk to rather than this small, chattering girl. As soon as Mr. Pat got back, he'd go visit Tommy Liang to share the good news about his job. Chinatown wasn't far.

"I'm glad you'll be my neighbor," Annie said, hopping from one cobblestone to another. "I just knew it when I saw you yesterday. Will you come meet Mama soon?"

"Sure, if I can get time away from my duties," Nick said, feeling important. "How is your mother?"

Annie bent down, wrapped her arms around Shakespeare's neck, and giggled as he licked her face. "All

65

right, I guess. She's been cleaning floors and doing fine sewing for some ladies who live in big houses up on Nob Hill. But with the baby coming, she only wants to do sewing. It's hard for her to walk up the steep hills now, so I'm her delivery girl."

Then in a voice so low Nick could barely hear, she added, "But the jar is getting awfully light."

The jar. Nick didn't need to ask Annie what that meant. Gran had kept a money jar on the top shelf in the kitchen. He didn't remember that it had ever been heavy. Sometimes, when Gran did some extra laundry or sold some eggs, she let him open it and drop the coins in one by one.

After Pa left, Nick discovered that Gran had another, secret hiding place for money. One evening, Gran had reached into the back of a drawer and pulled out two faded white gloves wrapped in tissue paper.

"I wore these gloves the day I married your grandfather," she told Nick, slipping her fingers partway into one of them. The glove no longer fit Gran's rough, work-worn hand.

Gran drew out a few bills and some coins. "Not that I ever meant to be mean about keeping things hidden from your father, you understand," she said, patting the small glove gently. "But my own mama told me a girl should always try to put a penny or two aside for herself and her babies. 'A penny that won't ever get drunk.' That's how she put it."

Gran's secret stash hadn't lasted long. She'd bought Nick the cap he still had. And the money had helped tide them over until they found work on Mr. Hank's farm. On that last day, Gran had given Mrs. Turner one quarter to pass on to Nick. Two bits. The coin was probably all that was left.

Nick reached into the pockets of his new pants. He'd been careful to take his two special coins out of the old pants and put them in his new ones.

He wondered if Annie and her mother were getting enough to eat. Once the baby came, it wouldn't be easy for Mrs. Sheridan to have time to do enough fine sewing to pay their rent. Nick's hands closed around the quarters, one coin in each pocket. But then he let go.

"Well, good night, Annie of the North Star. Maybe we'll see you tomorrow," he said. "Shakespeare and I have work to do."

"Come on, boy, time for bed." Shakespeare padded downstairs ahead of him, tail sweeping the steps like a golden broom.

"I've never had a dog before," Nick told him. Shake pricked up his ears, almost, Nick thought, as if he could understand. "We didn't have any pets. Not that you're mine, exactly. But we can be friends."

Once, when he was about seven, he'd begged to keep a kitten when Mr. Greene's brown tabby had a litter. But Gran had shaken her head, and Nick had known not to ask again.

Outside Mr. Pat's locked office door was a small room, furnished with an old sofa, a bedroll on the floor, a bookcase, and a table with a pitcher of water and some bread, cheese, and fruit. A narrow hallway led to a toilet and sink.

"The guest room," Mr. Pat had announced with a flourish when he'd showed it to Nick the night before. "I hope you'll find it to your liking, young sir. Of course, it's not nearly as grand as the Palace Hotel. Not even a curtain on the window, I'm afraid."

68

"Mr. Pat, is that you?" Nick had stood before a small photograph of a family on the top of the bookcase. It was a formal, old-fashioned portrait. The parents looked kind but serious. But the boy was slightly out of focus. Even though the mother had her arm around her son's shoulders to keep him steady, he must have moved at the last second.

Nick had felt in his pockets and touched his two quarters. He wished he still had the photograph of his mother. But Mr. Hank had been harsh. He'd sent for Mr. Kelly to haul Nick off to the orphanage without even giving him a chance to sort through Gran's belongings. Nick sometimes imagined that maybe little Rebecca and her mother had found it. They might even be keeping it for him, thinking that sooner or later, he'd turn up in the fields once again.

"Is that me in the photograph?" Mr. Pat asked, pulling blankets out of a cupboard and looking over his shoulder. "Yes, indeed. Poor Mother, bless her soul. Try as she might, she couldn't keep me still."

He turned back, his voice muffled by the blankets piled in his arms. "They never did get out from Boston to see the store. Now, then, I think these will keep you warm, Nicholas."

On Monday, Nick's first night with Mr. Pat, Shakespeare had bounded onto the corner of the tattered green sofa, yawned, stretched, and broken into a wide doggie grin.

"Any room for me?" Nick asked, grinning back. Mr. Pat had warned him that Shakespeare might not be too keen on sharing his favorite spot in the entire world.

"I hope you won't mind a bedroll," he'd said. "Later, once he gets to know you, perhaps Shakespeare will consent to your taking over the sofa. But he's a creature of habit. He'd probably just plop down on top of you. I'm not sure how well you'd sleep with a sixty-pound dog on your chest, panting into your face at all hours."

Tonight, with Mr. Pat gone, Nick expected Shakespeare to go straight to his place on the sofa again. Instead, as Nick stretched out on his blankets, the dog stood over him, legs apart, breathing hard. His chocolate eyes gazed into Nick's. He whined low in his throat.

"What's wrong? Do you miss Mr. Pat already?"

69

Nick scratched the dog's head and pulled gently on one ear. "Don't worry. I'll keep you safe."

Nick stared up at the ceiling.

"I'm here, Gran," he whispered out loud. "Safe. Safe in San Francisco. I even have a job and a place to stay, for now, anyway. Mr. Pat might keep me on if I take good care of Shakespeare and his treasures while he's away. So you don't need to worry about me."

Nick frowned. Well, it really was too soon to tell what would happen with Mr. Pat Patterson. He was such an unusual sort of person. He seemed to streak through each day like the stars Nick and Gran had watched flash through the dark August sky—moving fast, almost too quick to see.

"I wonder if Mr. Pat took me on only because it was convenient. After all, I showed up at just the right time. He needed to go away and didn't want to be bothered to take you with him," Nick said, sitting up on the bedroll and addressing Shake. "Maybe, come Thursday, he'll decide to send me on my way."

Shakespeare didn't seem to be listening. He whined, settled himself to the floor with a heavy sigh, and then after a minute got up again. The dog's nails clicked as he walked across to the stairs. He stood for a minute, listening, then trotted back to Nick.

"Settle down, boy. You're making me nervous. I'm trying to sort things out," Nick told him. He kept one hand on the dog's head, scratching idly.

70

It did seem to be a good sign that Mr. Pat was taking a chance on him. After all, not everyone would let a strange boy keep watch, even if the office and the shop were locked up tightly. And he had bought Nick those clothes.

Nick yawned. "What do *you* think, Shakespeare? Will Mr. Pat keep me on?"

Shake tilted his head, his ears pricking up at attention. He wagged his tail, which Nick decided was a good sign.

"Well, at least I know *you* like me, Shake. And I sure would love to learn this business. Did you see those folks who came in today to buy newspapers and magazines?" Nick went on, yawning again. "Mr. Pat said they were poets, writers, and newspaper reporters. It would be something to get to know people like that."

As he thought about the shop upstairs, Nick's sleepiness seemed to evaporate. He suddenly felt as jumpy as Shakespeare.

What if someone tried to break in? Would Nick be able to hear noises from down here in the basement? Would Shakespeare?

Nick peered into the darkness. Shakespeare had finally hopped up to his usual place on the sofa. He seemed asleep, but when he noticed Nick, he gave a few gentle wags of his tail.

Then, unexpectedly, he jumped off the sofa and paced around the room again, making the same whining

71

sound deep in his throat. Finally he curled up on the floor next to Nick and put his head on his paws.

"That's it, boy," Nick said, throwing his arm around the dog. "Everything's going to be all right. Let's go to sleep now."

CRACK

BOOM

Nick woke suddenly, with no idea where he was.

The light was dim, but it was morning. Early morning. Half asleep, Nick felt confused. His first thoughts flew to Gran. Where was she? Had he missed the bell calling Mr. Hank's workers to the fields?

Then, more awake, Nick realized where he was. Still, something *was* wrong. A deep, horrible rumbling. A high-pitched whine. That, at least, made sense. Shakespeare! Yes, he was in Mr. Pat's basement. The dog must need to go out.

Nick tried to pull himself up. *Bam!* He was thrown back onto the floor. And then the floor itself began to twist, shake, roll. The room erupted into a sick, violent motion.

CRASH

RUMBLE

CRACK

Nick's world shifted. Fast, faster. Everything began shaking faster than Nick could take in. He felt tiny, like an ant caught in a tumble of motion.

Nick saw things fly through the air, though his mind couldn't make sense of it.

First the table. The table shook and turned over. The water pitcher shot across the room and shattered, splashing water everywhere.

The bookcase in the corner toppled over, sending books and the photograph of Mr. Pat and his family crashing to the floor.

Something hit Nick's head. Plaster from the ceiling. From somewhere beyond his little room he heard rumblings, thunder-like roars, cracklings.

Get out. I need to get out. The building's falling down.

Shakespeare! Nick tried to shout the dog's name, but his voice didn't seem to work. He tried to find him, to stand, but he couldn't control his body.

SLAM

He fell back. His elbow banged hard.

The room trembled. Floor, ceiling, walls, objects, everything seemed to be dancing, rolling, moving.

For a second, the shaking let up. Then it started in again, violent and more twisting. An image flashed through Nick's mind of Gran wringing clothes over the wash tin with her rough, strong hands. That was it. The earth was being wrung out of shape.

Nick shivered. He was in a tiny boat being tossed and rolled on a great stormy sea. At any second, a hole

73

would open and he would fall through. Fall through and disappear, disappear into black emptiness.

Nick cried out.

He'd never been so terrified. It wasn't like seeing a snake writhing toward him in the grass. Or even the fear of Pa's temper after a Saturday night in town. This was bigger. A terror of something enormous, violent, menacing, unknown. It was all happening so fast, Nick couldn't give it a name.

And then from somewhere, his brain coughed up a word.

Earthquake! He was in an earthquake.

Earthquakes. Miss Reedy had talked about earthquakes in California, something about the pieces of the earth, shifting deep underground. In a way, just naming it made Nick a little less scared.

Earthquake. The world's not really ending. It's an earthquake.

And then, in the next second, everything shifted again. The shaking stopped. The air, the ground went still.

Nick coughed. The little room was filled with dust. He didn't know how long the fierce trembling had lasted. Thirty seconds? A full minute?

I'm alive, he thought. *I'm still alive.*

"Shakespeare?" Nick called.

Nick looked around, suddenly panicked. "Shake? Here, boy!"

The room seemed empty. Then all at once Nick heard a scuffling noise. In the gray light he saw Shakespeare emerge from behind the sofa.

The dog's dark eyes looked bright and wild. He planted his feet far apart, as though trying to steady himself. His long, feathery tail was tucked down between his legs. Suddenly Shake raised his muzzle and howled once. Then he barked at the air and ran toward the stairway.

Nick's knees were shaking so hard he didn't think he could walk. He fumbled, half crawling, across the dim, dusty room. At the top of the stairs, the door had flown open. Before Nick could stop him, Shake had darted out into the street.

"No, wait! Shakespeare, come back. Here, boy," Nick yelled.

He's looking for Mr. Pat, Nick thought, springing into action.

Nick reached the street. Shakespeare was nowhere to be seen.

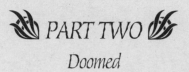 *PART TWO*
Doomed

The smoke of San Francisco's burning
was a lurid tower visible a hundred miles
away. And for three days and nights this
lurid tower swayed in the sky, reddening
the sun, darkening the day, and filling
the land with smoke. . . . Before the
flames, throughout the night, fled tens of
thousands of homeless ones. . . .

—Jack London,
"Story of an Eyewitness"

AFTERSHOCKS

"Shakespeare?" Nick called. "Shake. Here, boy!"

Jackson Street was empty and suddenly still. Nick looked up and down. He couldn't see anyone, not a dog or another person. Nick had a terrible thought: What if everyone else in the city got swallowed up?

He shivered and stuck his hands in his pockets. Yes, the coins were still there. And then all at once he missed Gran so much it hurt. He could almost hear her voice. "Land's sake, that felt like the earth was no more than a rat a little dog got hold of and tried to shake to death. But now let's get to work and right things."

That's what I should do, Nick told himself. *Get to work and right things.*

But it was hard to move, hard to trust that the shaking wouldn't begin again and throw him down.

Nick heard a cry.

"Come on, Tim. Don't fuss. Keep up now," a

woman scolded. A family of five or six emerged from a nearby doorway and began to rush toward Montgomery Street. The smallest boy trotted behind his mother, bawling loudly.

I'm not alone, Nick realized with relief. Other people had made it, too. And Jackson Street was still here. There were bricks in the road and shattered glass from broken windows littering the sidewalk. But at least in this small corner of the city, things looked fixable. The solid brick buildings were standing.

He shook his head to try to clear it. He had to think. He had to find Shakespeare. Where would the big dog go?

Nick looked toward Montgomery Street. That was the way Mr. Pat liked to walk downtown. Yes, he should go there first. Shake might have gone the same way out of habit.

"Is that your father's shop, son?" a police officer yelled to Nick as he ran past. "Better get those valuables out of sight. We'll have looters out soon, mark my words."

"Yes, sir."

Well, something else had changed. He didn't look like a runaway anymore. Nick tried the front door of the store. It was still locked. But that didn't matter. The shining plate glass window was gone. Sweeping bits of glass away, Nick climbed through the empty frame.

"I'll just grab the most valuable objects and hide

them, then go find Shakespeare," Nick said out loud. He didn't know why. Maybe just to break the eerie silence in the deserted store. Nick looked closely at the clock on the wall. It had stopped at exactly 5:12. Early morning.

Most people had probably been home in bed. A few hours later, the streets would have been bustling with people, carts, automobiles, and horses. It was lucky the quake had struck so early. He didn't like to think of horses rearing and panicking and running wild with fear in the crowded streets.

"Mr. Pat will be so upset," Nick said to himself, looking at the rubble around him.

The neat shelves of magazines and paper journals had toppled, spilling everything across the floor. Every glass case and window was shattered.

81

"Mr. Pat's inkwells!" Nick began to pick his way across the floor.

"Ouch!" Something sharp made him stop. Glass. Nick looked down at his stockinged feet. He'd forgotten all about his shoes. He'd been about to head to Market Street without them. He wasn't thinking straight.

Walking more carefully, Nick found a paper sack Mr. Pat used to wrap up purchases. As quickly as he could, he filled it with the best pens and inkwells. Some of the ink-wells had been smashed, but a few still looked perfect.

I should try to save more, Nick thought, looking frantically at the broken glass, the upturned display cases, and the merchandise strewn across the floor.

But he felt torn. He should go—now! He should be out looking for Shakespeare. What would Mr. Pat want him to do first?

Nick couldn't fit anything else into the sack. At least he had grabbed the best.

Trying not to get cut on the broken glass, Nick made his way back and climbed out again, the bag banging against his leg. In the little room downstairs, Nick stashed the treasures behind the tattered green sofa. For now, he hoped, the bag would be safe.

He was almost up the stairs again when he looked down at his feet. His mind was still fuddled. Everything was taking so long. He was wasting so much time.

He'd forgotten his shoes again.

On Montgomery Street, Nick joined a flow of people. Everyone seemed to be heading toward Market Street.

Above the jagged line of the tall city buildings, the early morning sky seemed almost as blue as in Texas. That surprised Nick. He hadn't been here long, but he'd already gotten used to the cool, foggy weather.

And so it seemed especially strange that today—of all days—should be sunny. The earthquake had been so violent and sudden. Nick wouldn't have been surprised to find himself in the midst of a terrible storm, with thunder, lightning, and howling winds.

Instead, it was clear and pleasant, without a trace of the usual damp fingers of fog. Nick shook his head, like a dog shaking water off its coat. It didn't help. His arms and legs ached, bruised from when he'd fallen. He felt fuzzy, off balance. He rubbed his elbow, which still hurt from when he'd banged it.

Nick put one foot in front of the other and concentrated on walking. He jumped at a shout behind him.

"Out of my way, boy," growled a man dragging a trunk. "I'm heading for the Ferry Building. We're gettin' out of this city before anything else happens."

The trunk scraped along the cobblestones, the man huffing with its weight. Just behind him, a small woman with a pinched white face was trying to run while she held a birdcage containing a fluttering yellow canary. "Wait for me, Amos. Poor Jerry here is twittering his head off."

Nick watched men, women, and children stream out of buildings and fill the streets. Some people were weighed down with heavy bags and boxes. Others carried odd, surprising objects—bulky paintings in gilded frames, kittens in birdcages, teakettles and dolls.

Beside Nick walked a man still wearing only a nightshirt, his thin legs poking out like white sticks. His wife had on a long dressing gown, a fancy white hat with long feathers perched precariously on her head. The couple had probably raced out of their house as soon as the earthquake stopped, Nick realized. They'd just left their beds for the street and grabbed the first thing that came to hand.

Just like me, Nick thought. *I forgot my own shoes.*

▥▥▥▥▥

Nick reached Market Street. Without knowing exactly why, he turned right, toward the Palace Hotel. When it came in sight, he breathed a sigh of relief. It looked magnificent. Nick could almost imagine the rich, fancy ladies and gentlemen inside.

When they'd walked past the day before, Mr. Pat had pointed to it and said, "It's the grandest hotel in America, Nicholas. The pride of San Francisco."

Almost without knowing it, Nick spoke out loud. "The Palace survived!"

A short, thick man with white hair turned to Nick. "Survived, did you say? Of course the Palace survived! Why, that building was designed to withstand earthquakes, son. The brick walls are two feet thick, and there's three thousand tons of iron in just those seven stories."

"How . . . how do you know?"

"Helped build it, now, didn't I? And I was here in 1875 when it opened," the man said, straightening his shoulders. He seemed to look past Nick. "October second, it was. Gleaming white marble, crystal chandeliers. I remember they had a grand banquet, but—"

"What about now? Will the Palace be all right?" Nick interrupted impatiently. The earthquake was over. The Palace looked fine. Nothing could be worse than what had just happened.

But before the man could answer, someone strode up to him and stopped short. "Bill, is that you?"

"Hullo, Mike!" The white-haired man next to Nick shook his friend's hand and slapped him on the shoulder. "You're safe. Glad to see you. Everything all right?"

The man called Mike sighed and shook his head, sending a spatter of plaster and dust into the air. "I just came from south of the Slot. Bad news there. The Valencia Street Hotel's collapsed. Do you know it?"

"One of those cheap wooden boardinghouses, ain't it? Built on filled land, like those others—Brunswick Hotel, Nevada House." Bill shook his head. "Restin' on nothin' but swamp, those places are."

"You've nailed it," Mike said. Nick thought the man's face looked as white as the plaster in his hair. "Those poor creatures in the Valencia Street Hotel didn't have a chance. Four stories just collapsed into the swamp. Killed. I dunno how many. Maybe hundreds."

"Some of them on the bottom probably drowned, I'll wager," said Bill in a low voice. He cleared his throat. "You headed to the ferry, Mike? I'll go with you."

Then he turned to Nick. "You should go home and tell your parents to leave now, kid."

"But why? The earthquake's over." Nick's head was spinning. He couldn't believe what the man had said about the Valencia Street Hotel. He knew that building. After he'd met Tommy, he'd gone by there looking for work and a place to sleep. If it hadn't been

85

for Mr. Pat, he might have been sleeping there or in some alley south of the Slot. *I could have sunk into the swamp,* Nick thought. *It might have been me.*

Mike pointed. "See over there?"

Nick followed the man's finger. "That puff of smoke? I don't understand."

"Fire. Probably got started from a broken gas main or sparks from stoves," said Bill.

"There are lots of fire stations," said Nick. "And firemen with their fast horses and long hoses. I've seen them."

Mike shrugged. "Maybe. Let's hope you're right, kid. Friend of mine told me that Dennis Sullivan, the fire chief, is hurt bad. Part of the California Hotel toppled off and tore through the station where he and his wife were sleeping."

Bill cast another glance at the Palace Hotel. "Let's hope someone else besides Sullivan has water and a plan. Otherwise, we're in for the worst."

The two men walked off before Nick had a chance to ask: What was the worst?

Woof. Woof!

Nick jumped at the sound. He turned. But it wasn't Shakespeare. Instead, he saw a large black dog with a white spot on his face barking at a kitten on a man's shoulder.

86

"People, dogs, cats, birds—everywhere," Nick said to himself. "I'll never find him in this crowd."

Everyone seemed to be heading straight down Market Street toward the Ferry Building. The ferry. Nick snatched at the idea. Mr. Pat had gone in that direction last night. Shakespeare had probably gone with him in the past. Maybe that was where he'd made for.

Nick joined the wave of people. It felt strange to be walking in the middle of the wide avenue, usually so crowded with cable cars, wagons, and automobiles. Ahead stood the Ferry Building's tall tower, boasting four giant clocks, one on each side.

Just a few days ago Nick seemed to be the only one without a place to be—the only person out of place. Now everyone had that same look he must have had—lost, uncertain, scared.

No wonder. This morning the solid earth had twisted, danced, and rolled. Nick felt a little dizzy. It was almost as if just thinking about the earthquake took him back inside it.

All at once the earth did begin to tremble. Nick came to a halt, planted his feet wide. He was shaking. Around him he could hear shouts and screams.

"Oh, no! Help me!"

"It's coming again!"

An older woman near him with a deep, musical voice called out, "Don't panic. It's just a strong aftershock."

Aftershock. It was like a bad dream that returned night after night.

"Are you all right, young man?"

Nick looked up into the woman's lined face. "Is it dangerous?"

"It's just the earth settling. I expect we'll have many of them," she said. Then she added, "But, dearie, make sure you keep away from walls and the sides of buildings. You don't want loose bricks collapsing on top of you."

As he drew close to the pier, Nick's heart sank. This was impossible. He'd never find Shakespeare here. The pier was packed with people everywhere he turned.

The crowd surged forward suddenly, and a shout went up. "Here's the ferry now!"

I could go, too, if I wanted, Nick realized.

He didn't have to go back to Mr. Pat's store. He could escape San Francisco right now. Maybe the earthquake was a sign he didn't belong here after all.

For a second Nick closed his eyes, shutting out everything else. He wished he knew what to do. He imagined himself on the ferry, turning back to look at the tall buildings as they shrank smaller and smaller across the bay.

He could make his way to another city or turn himself in at some orphanage. Mr. Pat Patterson wouldn't miss him. But what about Shakespeare?

He's just a dog. Mr. Pat's dog. He's not even mine, Nick told himself.

Nick opened his eyes and sighed.

He took two steps and bumped into a man loaded down with belongings. "Hey, watch it!" the man cried. "You're headed in the wrong direction, kid."

"Sorry," Nick mumbled automatically, pulling his cap down close over his unruly hair.

Nick broke into a trot. He pushed through the crowd and headed back to Jackson Street.

FORGOTTEN

Nick's heart sank when he reached Montgomery and Jackson. No dog in sight.

"Shakespeare!" he called. He tried to conjure up the dog from his imagination, tried to will him to suddenly appear on the street, tail wagging so hard his whole body shook.

"Shakespeare," he shouted, louder. Nick was about to turn onto Jackson Street when he heard something. It wasn't a bark, though. Someone was calling his name.

"Nick!"

Annie appeared in the doorway of her rooming house, her cheeks streaked with tears and dirt.

Nick sprinted toward her. He felt ashamed. He'd run right by the rooming house earlier without even giving a thought to little Annie Sheridan and her mother.

A large red bump protruded on Annie's forehead.

She hiccuped. "Mama needs help, Nick. The ceiling fell on her."

Nick's heart pounded. He thought about the fire chief and his wife. "You're hurt, too," said Nick, reaching out his hand to touch Annie's forehead.

Annie pulled away. "Where were you? Why didn't you come sooner? I thought you were my friend."

"I—I'm sorry, Annie . . . ," Nick stammered.

"Come now," Annie urged, turning toward the door. "You are not a very good rescuer, Nick."

"It'll be all right, Annie," Nick said, feeling stung. He tried to sound sure, but his words sounded half-hearted even to him.

The first thing Nick noticed as they climbed the rickety stairs was how quiet it was. No talking or laughter. No children crying, or smells of cooking, or someone playing a fiddle.

There was an eerie, deserted feel to everything. Nick figured the other tenants had been so frightened they'd thought only of themselves. No one had bothered to stop to look for people left behind.

"Annie, do you have any other friends or some family you and your mother can stay with now?"

Annie shook her head. "Just Mama. We came on the train from back east. We came to wait for Daddy."

On the first landing, Annie stopped and pointed to a doorway. All at once Nick felt the floorboards tremble. Another aftershock.

91

Annie gave a little cry. Nick reached out to hold on to her in case she fell. But the shaking passed quickly.

Annie looked beyond Nick at the door, which stood ajar. "In there," she said. "I fell out of bed and couldn't get up. I think I bumped my head, or maybe I fell back to sleep. I'm not sure."

"What happened next?" Nick moved toward the door.

"When I woke up and yelled for Mama, she was still on the bed. Real still. I think . . . I think the ceiling is on top of her."

Nick stopped, his hand on the doorknob. He hoped Annie wouldn't notice how his hand was trembling. "You wait here, Annie. Let me go first."

She shook her head and fixed him with her startling eyes.

Nick pushed open the door and peered inside. Annie was right. Part of the ceiling had fallen across the bed. There were boards and beams sticking out all over. He could just make out a figure huddled under a blue blanket.

Nick's heart was pounding so loud it made his head hurt. He kept Annie behind him, pushing his shoulder in front of her so she couldn't see.

"Hello? Mrs. Sheridan? Ma'am, can you hear me?"

Nick drew closer to the bed. *Please be all right,* he breathed silently. *Please.*

"Mrs. Sheridan, wake up," he called, louder this time. "Mrs. Sheridan!"

A faint groan came from the bed. Annie's mother moved her head.

"Mama!" Annie cried. "Mama, talk to me."

Under the rubble Nick caught sight of a slender white hand with a thin gold ring on one finger.

"Annie, here's her hand," Nick said, relief flooding through him. "Hold on to it and squeeze it hard while I see about getting all this off her. Then maybe she'll be able to talk."

Nick set to work pulling off plaster and wood with both hands. The debris had left large gaps as the pieces fell. He thought there was a chance she hadn't actually been crushed under all this rubble.

Nick uncovered the top of the bed first. "There, that's better."

Annie drew closer and threw her arms around her mother's neck. It seemed to Nick the woman on the bed looked young, for a mother, anyway. Or maybe he'd just gotten used to Gran.

"Mama!" Annie said urgently.

Mrs. Sheridan opened her eyes. Nick could see where Annie got her large eyes. Unlike Annie's, though, her mother's were both the same color—a soft, light blue. Her face was pale and drained. She was covered with dirt, dust, and flecks of paint.

"Are you all right, ma'am?" Nick asked.

Mrs. Sheridan turned to Annie. She tried to smile. "I don't know. I think so. What about you, Little Big Eyes?"

Annie burst into tears and buried her face on her mother's neck.

"My name is Nick, ma'am. I'm a neighbor. I'll see about getting you out." Nick ran to the foot of the bed, where a section of the ceiling had fallen over Mrs. Sheridan's ankles and calves. "It looks like you're pinned under this, but it's not quite touching your legs. Can you wiggle your toes?"

"Yes," Mrs. Sheridan said. "That's not what hurts."

Annie was brushing dirt and specks of plaster from her mother's hair. "Mama, the baby? Is the baby all right?"

"Yes, I think so. I can feel it moving. But something hit my right side." Annie's mother clutched her daughter's hand. "Are you sure you're all right, Annie? You were so quiet."

Nick swallowed hard, feeling guilty all over again. Annie might have been badly hurt.

"Well, Annie does have that bump on her head as big as an egg," Nick told Mrs. Sheridan. "But I expect she'll be talking away as much as ever any minute now, won't you, Annie of the North Star?"

As he spoke, Nick studied the pile of rubble. Carefully he worked at clearing it away, piece by piece. Before long he was done, except for a section of wallboard and plaster that lay across Annie's mother's legs.

"Ma'am, if I can lift this, do you think you can wriggle out from under?"

"Well, I . . . I can try." Annie's mother looked doubtful. What if she couldn't walk?

Nick remembered how Gran used to rub her legs to "get the blood flowing" after she'd sat awhile. He called Annie over.

"Annie, I'm going to use a lever to lift this big piece of wall," he told her. "Come and rub your mother's legs so she can move them."

Nick hoped his idea would work. He grunted, trying to lift the piece as high as he could. Finally, with Annie's help, Mrs. Sheridan was able to pull first one leg free and then the other.

95

Nick and Annie helped her to sit up on the edge of the bed. She was weak and dizzy.

"Can you walk, ma'am?" asked Nick. "We'll support you."

Mrs. Sheridan leaned, putting weight on her feet. "Yes, I think I can. Nothing's broken. Except—ah, my right side. It hurts, especially when I move."

Suddenly they felt another shake. The building trembled and creaked.

"Aftershocks, Annie," her mother whispered. She shook her head and held her side. "Sorry . . . it hurts to talk."

"Mrs. Sheridan, I know it's painful. But we can't stay here much longer." Nick glanced at the ceiling. He didn't like the look of the gaping hole above their heads. "This building isn't safe. It could collapse any minute. Everyone else has gotten out."

"All right. Just leave Annie and me alone a few moments so we can dress. But then . . . but then where will we go? We have no family here."

Nick hesitated. He wondered what Mr. Pat would say if he came home to find Annie and her mother living in his store. Nick wasn't sure. He'd just have to make Mr. Pat understand.

"Ma'am, I'm at the stationer's shop nearby," Nick told her. "It's a small brick building. And it stood up to the quake real well. You'll be safe there."

A few minutes later, they were making their way out of the room and down the stairway of the rooming house.

"Be careful on this step. There's a hole right here," Nick warned. He glanced up at the floors above. He didn't want to be caught here by falling debris.

Every once in a while, Mrs. Sheridan breathed sharply and clutched her side. Nick wondered if she'd broken a rib. That had happened to Pa once. He'd complained for a week or more. But Annie's mother, he could tell, was trying hard to bear the pain in silence.

As they reached the sidewalk, they heard a crash from inside.

"Wait, we forgot! We didn't bring any of our things," said Annie suddenly.

Annie's mother shook her head. "Oh, Annie. It's not safe. Maybe later."

"What about the picture of Daddy?" Annie asked. "Will you get it for me, Nick?"

"You heard that crash, Annie. It's too dangerous," her mother said firmly.

Annie bit her lip. Nick saw tears fill her bright eyes. He looked back at the building.

"Where is it, Mrs. Sheridan? I can race up."

"No. It's too—"

"I'm quick. Was it on a dresser?" Nick interrupted. He was halfway to the door.

Mrs. Sheridan nodded. "Everything is on the floor now, I'm sure. Please be careful."

Nick pattered up the stairs softly. "Just think of how a cat walks," he told himself.

He tiptoed across the landing and entered the room. Annie and her mother didn't own much—a few books, a sewing basket, and some clothes. But he could barely pick out these items from the dirt and plaster and boards that covered the floor.

Nick felt the room sway a little. He dropped down to all fours and began to crawl. But he saw nothing that looked like a photograph. He didn't see the money jar Annie's mother kept, either.

97

What if I don't find it? he thought. Annie's heart would break.

He spotted a small cloth doll and grabbed it. The dresser had tumbled to the floor and broken into pieces.

And then, out of the corner of his eye, he spied something glinting under a shattered pitcher. He crawled over and reached under the broken porcelain. The glass frame had shattered, and the picture was covered with dust.

But this was it. Annie's parents, with Annie a baby in her mother's arms. Staring at it, Nick thought that it seemed worth the risk.

98

"Daddy's picture *and* my doll! Oh, Nick, you're my friend for life!" Annie exclaimed as they slowly made their way along Jackson Street.

"Annie, you've told Nick that five times in the last three minutes," her mother whispered with a weak smile. It was hard for her to talk.

Nick adjusted his arm to better support Annie's mother as she walked. "Mrs. Sheridan, just a few more steps and we'll be there."

He looked up and down the street. "I kept hoping Shakespeare would be right here waiting for me," Nick said.

As they approached Mr. Pat's store, Nick realized the door leading to the basement office stood open. He must have forgotten to close it when he left.

He'd lost track of time. Had the earthquake been two hours ago? Three? Mrs. Sheridan sagged a little against Nick's arm. He was afraid she might faint.

"We're almost there, Mama," whispered Annie.

Suddenly they felt another shake, stronger and more powerful than before. Annie looked back at the rooming house. "It's happening again."

Nick looked, too, and shivered.

At the top of the stairs, Nick heard a rustling noise. He thought of the police officer's warning about looters.

"Wait here!" he said. "Let me go first. Someone might be in there."

Nick tiptoed down a few steps, peering into the semi-darkness of the basement.

Nick heard a thumping noise. He saw something move toward him fast, then, in a rush, he felt paws against his chest. He almost fell over.

"Shake. Hey, boy! You came home!"

The Last Wagon

"Did you say your father owns the store upstairs?" Annie's mother asked. She flinched and held on to her side. Nick righted the sofa and helped her get settled.

"Oh, no, ma'am. I'm just watching it for Mr. Pat Patterson, the owner, while he's away," Nick explained.

He found a blanket on the floor and tucked it behind Mrs. Sheridan's head. "I'm sorry you're hurting so bad. Once my pa had an accident plowing. Gran said he must have cracked a rib. He said the sharp pain was worse than a toothache."

"I think you may be right," she said. "But as long as my baby isn't hurt, I don't mind. I can just rest here a few days and I'm sure I'll be fine."

Nick doubted she'd be better so quickly. He suspected Annie's mother was hurting more than she let on. Pa, Nick remembered, had just about driven Gran crazy with his complaints. "Oh, stop carrying on, John,"

she'd finally snapped, "or I'll crack the other side."
Then she'd winked at Nick to show she hadn't really
meant it.

Now Nick tried to think what Gran would have
done to make Mrs. Sheridan comfortable. He found a
glass and one jug of water that hadn't been broken. He
was pouring out water for Annie and her mother when
he was startled by a sharp bark.

Annie giggled. "Nick, you forgot to give your dog
some water. Look, he's sitting up so nicely, just wagging
his tail and hoping you'll notice him."

"So he is. All right, boy." Nick found a small, un-
broken bowl and watched while Shakespeare lapped
noisily, wagging his tail the whole time.

His dog. Annie had called Shake his. Mr. Greene
had kept dogs on his farm. But Nick had always been
afraid of them. They were mean, noisy creatures that
snarled and bared sharp yellow teeth whenever he came
near the farmhouse where Mr. Greene lived.

"Nick, are you here alone, then?" Mrs. Sheridan
wanted to know. "Where did Mr. Patterson go?"

"He left last night. He went to Oakland on business. . . ." Nick took off his cap and pushed his hair out
of his eyes. "I . . . I wish I knew if the earthquake hit
Oakland. I don't even know where Mr. Pat is."

"Don't worry, Nick, Mr. Pat will come back," Annie
piped up. "Remember, my daddy says you can't give
up believing."

Annie cradled the photograph in her lap, next to her doll. She sure talked about her father a lot. Over Annie's head, Nick met Mrs. Sheridan's eyes. He could find no answer there to the question he wanted to ask.

"I hope you're right, Annie," Nick said, reaching down to scratch Shakespeare's head. "Mr. Pat will be back, won't he, boy?"

Not long after, Mrs. Sheridan dropped off to sleep. Nick wished Annie would take a nap, too. Her chattering was back—she must be feeling better—and he was afraid she would wake her mother. Not only that, his ears were getting sore from listening.

Annie curled up on a blanket on the floor. Two minutes later, her head shot up.

"I don't really take naps, Nick, remember? Besides, I'm thirsty again," she announced. "And hungry. Can I have something to eat? I never ate breakfast because of the earthquake, and that feels like hours and hours ago."

"Let's see what I can find." Nick gave Annie another drink of water. Then he turned to look at the rubble of overturned shelves and cabinets. "Mr. Pat left me some bread, if I can find it."

Annie was rummaging, too. She held up a can of soup. "I found something. Let's have soup! I like hot soup."

Nick shook his head. "No soup, Annie."

"Why not?" Annie squinted at the can. "It's a little dented, but it will be all right. I can help you find the can opener."

"It's not that, Annie. We can't use the stove. I heard a man say the gas mains are broken. That means it's dangerous to use stoves now because it could start a fire."

Nick held the water jug in his hands. It wasn't enough to last until tomorrow. No water, no soup. He'd have to go out—or they would have to leave the safety of the little room.

Nick glanced again at Mrs. Sheridan. He wished he knew the right thing to do. Annie's mother didn't seem like she should be walking around the streets. If they could stay here until tomorrow, maybe Mr. Pat would be back to help.

But they couldn't stay without more water and something to eat.

Nick got an idea. "Here, Shake."

Shake planted himself on Nick's feet, looking up with friendly brown eyes, just as he'd done that first day. Nick bent down and scratched behind one floppy ear. Annie giggled, and Nick realized she was listening. He chose his words carefully.

"Now, Shakespeare, I have a job for you," he commanded. "I need you to stay with Annie and her mama for just a little bit while I go out."

For answer, Shakespeare barked once and broke into a wide smile.

"Out?" Annie put her hands on her hips. "Why do you get to go out? I want to do something, too. If I don't keep busy, I'll get all squirmy inside."

Nick pointed to the small bookcase. "You can help put Mr. Pat's books back on the shelves and make his things nice," he told her. "I won't be gone long. I just want to find us something to eat and drink. You can be in charge of Shake and take care of your mother, too."

"Well, all right. I do like being in charge." Annie's eyes glowed brightly, even in the dim light of the basement. "Where are you going, Nick?"

At first Nick was silent. Where *could* he go to find food or water?

"Chinatown. I'm going to Chinatown."

Nick walked down Montgomery to Washington Street, turned left at the corner, and then headed toward Chinatown. He caught an acrid smell in the air. He could see spirals of smoke in the distance, rising dark and thick above the crowded buildings.

Boom! Boom!

Nick jumped, startled.

"What's that sound?" he asked a man standing on the corner.

"Dynamite," the man answered, wiping beads of sweat from his face with his handkerchief. "That's why I'm dragging my trunk outta here."

Nick frowned. "What's the dynamite for?"

"Firemen are blowing up buildings in the fire's path to contain it, make a firebreak. Or at least they're trying to."

"Trying to?"

"Well, I tell you. I've done some mining in my day—used dynamite and explosives for years." The man shook his head and stuck his handkerchief in his pocket. "Now I just saw these firemen set a building on fire instead of bringing it to the ground. You got to be smart about it—you got to create obstacles for the fire, not feed the dang thing."

"Can't you help—show them how to do it?"

"I went up to one fellow, but he didn't listen. So that's it. I'm leaving while I can."

"My street still seems safe."

The man just shrugged. "But for how long?"

Nick kept on toward Chinatown, quickening his steps. The man's words echoed in his mind. *How long?*

San Francisco was an enormous, modern city. The firemen must know how best to stop the fires.

"Where you headed, kid?"

Nick stopped in his tracks. Right in front of him, a

policeman emerged from the door of a building. He was, Nick noticed, the opposite of Bushy Brows. *Skinny as a string bean,* Gran would have said.

"I . . . I just want to see a friend . . . in Chinatown."

"A friend?" scoffed the officer, rubbing a hand across the back of his neck. Nick stared at his feet. He hoped he wouldn't have to run from this man. He was sure to be faster than Bushy Brows. "You can't come into Chinatown now. We're starting to evacuate everyone here."

"Evacuate?"

"These flimsy wooden buildings don't stand a chance if fire spreads this way."

The man looked away to wave a wagon and a horse through. Nick saw his chance. He slipped by and then turned the next corner.

Evacuating. Dynamite. Nick cast quick glances at the sky. Yes, there was definitely more smoke now. He began to walk faster.

Chinatown was bustling with horses, wagons, and people scurrying here and there, hauling trunks and satchels. At first Nick wondered if he'd be able to recognize Tommy's store again.

And he might not have. But then he caught sight of Tommy, loading a box onto a wagon.

"Hullo, Tommy! Are you leaving now?"

Tommy stopped in surprise. For a moment he

seemed not to recognize Nick. Then he bowed and a smile lit his face. "Ah, the cotton boy. Hello, Nick. I hope you are not in trouble again."

Nick was about to answer when a man came out of the store, his arms full of bags and boxes. This must be Tommy's cousin.

Nick drew back a few steps. Maybe he shouldn't have come. He'd arrived at the wrong time. Tommy and his cousin were already packed up and ready to leave. There wouldn't be a chance to ask for help.

All at once Nick saw the cousin wave his hands and shout at Tommy. Tommy seemed to be arguing back, though Nick could not understand the words. Suddenly the older man pushed him aside, hopped onto the wagon, and motioned for the driver to go. There was a clatter of hooves on the cobblestones, and then they were gone.

Nick took a few steps toward Tommy. He could see tears fill his eyes. Tommy ducked his head and rushed inside.

Nick bit his lip. He stood still a minute and then followed Tommy into the store. It seemed empty at first.

"Tommy?"

Nick heard a noise and went to the back. Tommy was bent over a battered trunk, his fingers fumbling with one of its leather straps.

Nick shifted from one foot to the other. He hoped Tommy would speak first, but the older boy ignored him. "I . . . I'm glad to see you made it through the quake."

Still no answer. Tommy wasn't making it easy. Nick spoke softly. "Was that your cousin?"

All at once, like a cord snapping, Tommy straightened up and threw out his arms toward the shelves. His voice sounded flat and bitter. "Are you here for food again, Nick? I don't have much to give you. As you can see, the shelves are mostly empty. My cousin has taken the merchandise."

Nick flushed and took a step back. "It's . . . it's not for me. It's for a little girl and her mother. But I didn't just come to beg. I would've come to see you, anyway, to thank you. And to tell you I found a job—with Mr. Pat Patterson, a stationer on Jackson Street. He even gave me a place to stay."

Tommy shrugged, as if to say this had nothing to do with him.

"Tommy, I'm sorry. I really did want to come and see you again. But I don't understand. Why . . . why didn't your cousin take you in the wagon?"

"My cousin said he didn't have enough money for us both to ride." Tommy spat the words out quickly. "Wagonloads cost one hundred dollars right now. Everyone wants to get out."

"He's leaving you behind, just like that?"

"He said since I speak English and am an American,

I should be fine on my own." Tommy hung his head. "My father . . ."

Nick swallowed hard. Tommy's greedy cousin had used the earthquake as an excuse to take everything. *He walked away, just like Pa.*

Tommy ducked his head again so Nick couldn't see his face. After a minute he sighed and went to a shelf. "My cousin took all he could carry on the wagon. But he left these oranges behind."

He held out a bag to Nick, his voice softer now. "Take them. It's all right. And this jug of water, too."

"Why don't you come back to Jackson Street with me?" Nick urged as he struggled to balance the jug and the bulging sack of fruit. "There aren't any fires near there. I think the man who hired me will come back soon. He'll help us. You too."

Tommy shook his head. "No. I'll pull my trunk up Nob Hill along with the others who must walk."

"Where will you go?"

"I want to leave the city if I can."

"Will you go away?" Nick asked. "Will you try to find your mother?"

"In China?" Tommy shook his head. "No. But my father has distant relatives in Oakland. I will try to get there. For now, though, I will go to the Presidio, the army base. My neighbor said there may be a camp for Chinese set up there. It's a long walk."

He paused a minute, looking at the trunk. His shoulders slumped, and the anger seemed to drain out of his voice. "It won't be easy to drag my father's trunk alone. It would be better with two."

Nick stared at the trunk. Tommy was inviting him along, he realized. Maybe, after all, Tommy didn't just think he was a nuisance or another mean, teasing boy.

"I . . . I wish I could go with you, Tommy. But I can't. My boss might already be back."

"Back? What makes you think he'll come back?" Tommy asked. "He might be dead, or maybe he only cares about saving himself. He has known you just a few days. Why should he care or come back for you?"

Would Mr. Pat want to come back to the city? Would he even be able to get back in? Nick took off his cap and twisted it in his hands. His hair fell over his eyes, and he brushed it away.

"Well, you're right. He might not care about coming back for me," Nick said at last. "But he left his dog here. And there's his store, too. I think . . . I think those things matter to him."

Nick sighed. "Besides, I can't leave my neighbors. I should have gone to check on them earlier, and I didn't. I have to go back to them."

Nick didn't want to be like Tommy's cousin or Pa. He thought of the promise he'd made to himself after Pa left. *I won't do that. I won't ever walk away.*

Nick helped Tommy drag the trunk out of the store

to the sidewalk. Without a word, Tommy grabbed the handle. With a slight wave to Nick, he set out in a slow, awkward walk, joining the parade of people hurrying along the street.

Nick looked after him. Somehow, even among his neighbors, Tommy seemed so alone. Tommy was the first person who'd been kind to him in San Francisco. Nick was afraid to think what might happen to him. Even if the store itself wasn't destroyed by fire, Tommy would have no money to restock it or open it again.

Nick put down the sack and the jug of water. He stuck one hand in his pocket. His fingertips brushed against one of his coins. The coins were all he had, except for his cap, to remind him of Gran.

Nick thought of Rebecca and her mother. Folks who'd had so little. But they had given what they could out of kindness.

Nick dug his heel into the sidewalk and started to run. "Tommy, wait!"

The tall, thin figure ahead turned around. Nick pulled up next to him and, reaching into his pocket, drew out one silver quarter.

Nick grabbed Tommy's hand and pressed the quarter into it. "I'm sorry . . . about everything. This is for you. It's a special coin. It will give you luck."

Everyone Out

Good thing my arms are strong, Nick thought as he trotted back toward Jackson Street with his bulky load.

But a worry nagged at him. Oranges wouldn't do much to help Annie's hunger.

Maybe Mr. Pat would be back soon. Why, he might already be there. Nick could almost hear him exclaiming over Shakespeare and taking charge of getting Mrs. Sheridan to safety.

A blast of dynamite close by made him jump. Nick stopped to catch his breath. The sky was becoming a roiling mass of dark smoke. He coughed. Thick bits of ash flew everywhere, and his eyes hurt from the smoky air.

The fires were getting worse, not better. Nick remembered Bill, the white-haired man he'd met near the Palace Hotel. There'd better be water and a plan, he'd said. "Otherwise, we're in for the worst."

The worst.

Nick turned onto the familiar cobblestoned street with its solid redbrick buildings. He stopped and let out his breath in relief. The fire hadn't touched Mr. Pat's little neighborhood—at least not yet.

Woof!

Nick turned. Shakespeare must have been watching from the doorway. Now he bounded out, whining and wiggling with joy. He made frantic circles around Nick, his whole body wagging furiously. He hurled himself onto Nick's feet and barked, begging to be petted.

Nick laughed, put down the water and oranges, and ran his hands through Shake's silky fur. "You're glad enough to see me now. So don't run away again! Has Mr. Pat come home?"

A voice called out from the other side of the street. "Hullo, is that Shakespeare? Is Pat here?"

At the sound of his name, Shake turned in mid-air and sprang across the cobblestones. He planted himself in front of Ed Lind, who was just coming out of Hotaling's whiskey warehouse across the street.

"Hullo, Shake," Ed said, pulling affectionately at one of the dog's silky ears. "We really *will* have to call you Shake now, won't we, after that earthquake? Where's your master? I haven't seen him since this happened."

Nick came closer and shifted from one foot to the other. "He's gone."

"Gone?" Ed Lind looked up sharply at Nick's words.

"Oh, no! I didn't mean . . . ," Nick sputtered. "At least I hope not. Mr. Pat went to Oakland yesterday on business."

"Leave it to Pat to miss all the excitement. Now I remember—I met you the other day. What's your name again, son?"

"Nick. Nicholas Dray."

"Well, Nick, I wouldn't worry too much about Pat. Most likely he's having trouble getting back." He paused to glance at the sky, where dark columns of smoke covered the sun. "But you should leave now. It's not clear how long we can keep the block free of fire."

114

Nick gestured down the street. "I see lots of soldiers there. It looks like they're protecting that big government building. Can't they save Jackson Street, too?"

"Maybe, but we need water for the hoses, and the earthquake caused breaks in the water mains and other underground pipes." Ed Lind shook his head. "No one knows what's going to happen. You shouldn't take a chance."

Nick glanced over to Mr. Pat's store and its shattered, gaping windows.

"It's . . . it's not just me. I hope Mr. Pat won't be mad, but Annie Sheridan and her mother are staying with me. You know Annie, the girl from the rooming house. Her mother got hurt some in the earthquake and can't walk very well."

"All the more reason to go. I wish I could help, but I can't leave the warehouse." Ed Lind looked down the street. "Hold on. Here's the captain I need to talk to now."

He stepped out in front of a man in uniform.

"Captain! Stop a minute, will you? I'm Ed Lind, cashier for Hotaling's whiskey establishment here," said Ed all in a rush. "I've heard talk of dynamiting this block to make a firebreak. I'm begging you not to let it happen. For one thing, it won't work."

The captain raised his eyebrows in surprise. "Won't work?"

115

"This is a warehouse, sir. A whiskey warehouse." Ed leaned in close to make his point. "We've got five thousand barrels of liquor stored here."

The captain whistled. "Five thousand?"

"That's right, five thousand barrels of flammable liquid," Ed repeated. "Setting off dynamite on this block will create a powerful firestorm. The whole block will be an inferno. You'll destroy any chance you have of saving the Appraisers' Building."

Nick stepped closer to hear the captain's answer. The captain sighed and drew a hand over his forehead. His eyes looked bloodshot, and his face was streaked with soot. "I wish someone would give me some good news, Mr. Lind. As it is, every hour that goes by convinces me the city is doomed."

Nick shivered a little and buried his hands in Shake's soft fur.

"Chief Sullivan is on his deathbed," the captain went on. "The quake ruptured water mains and other pipes. A lot of these men wielding dynamite don't know what they're doing."

"All the more reason to give me a chance, sir," pleaded Ed. "I have a plan."

"A plan?"

"Yes. I'm prepared to get men to empty the warehouse of as much whiskey as we can. We'll roll the barrels a few blocks away to a place that's already been burned and blackened. The less liquor here, the better chance you have of saving your government building."

The captain frowned. "Where are you going to find these men of yours?"

"The docks. We'll round up every able-bodied man we can find," Ed told him. "We can pay a dollar an hour. Please, let us try."

"All right. You make a good case, Lind." The captain seemed to notice Nick for the first time. He took out a handkerchief, wiped his forehead, and heaved a sigh. "So, are you strong enough to lift whiskey barrels and roll them down the street? Or will you be pressing your fine dog there into service, the way they use those St. Bernard dogs in the Alps?"

Nick gulped. "I work in that building across the street. Shake and I will do what we can to help, sir."

The captain laughed. "Shake, huh? That dog is well named."

Nick watched the captain stride away down Jackson Street. Nick reached out and caught Ed Lind's elbow.

"Please, Mr. Lind, before you go, can I ask you a question? Where . . . where should I take Annie and her mother?"

"Well, the fires are moving slowly, but the wind makes everything unpredictable," Ed said thoughtfully. "You might be safe up the hill at Union Square. You could head there first and see what you find out. Can you get them that far?"

"I'll try," Nick replied, stooping to pick up the water jug and the oranges. He headed across the street.

Try. It was a word Gran had used a lot.

Just try, boy, that's all I ask of you, she'd tell him. For Gran, trying was just doing what had to be done, day in and day out. She didn't really think about any other way.

But Pa had looked trying in the face and turned his back. *Pa would've been on the first ferry out of San Francisco,* Nick thought. And Gran? Nick figured Gran would have been like Ed Lind, determined to save whatever little patch she had.

"Hey, Nick!" Ed Lind called.

117

Nick turned.

"Better start now. And don't come back," Ed warned. "You got that? Don't come back."

Just as Nick feared, Annie didn't want to go.

"This street isn't on fire. It looks just the same as always, except for the windows and all. I want to stay here, Nick," she pleaded, her big eyes wide with alarm. "What if Daddy comes back for Mama and me? If we leave, he'll never find us. Never. He'll look at the broken-down building and he'll think we . . . we . . ."

She couldn't go on. Tears welled in her eyes. Nick looked toward Annie's mother, dozing on the sofa, curled slightly like a cat. Her eyes were closed and her breath came slowly.

What happens if they won't go? If I can't get them out of the path of the fire?

Nick felt a flash of panic. He couldn't fail this time. Not like he'd failed before, with Gran. And not just Gran. When he stopped to think about it, Nick could count a lot of things he'd failed at. Or maybe, like Pa, he'd just not tried hard enough.

School, for one thing. He'd liked Miss Reedy all right. But except for writing lessons, he hadn't bothered to work all that hard. Arithmetic or reading wouldn't change much for a sharecropper's kid. Or at least that's what he'd told himself.

"Annie, we have to go to Union Square," Nick

118

repeated. He wished he knew the right thing to say. "It's just not safe here."

Annie's mother opened her eyes. She struggled to a sitting position, wincing. She held out her arms. "Annie."

Annie ran to her, burying her face in her mother's shoulder.

Mrs. Sheridan smoothed Annie's hair and nodded to Nick. "I want Annie and this new baby to be safe."

"Yes, ma'am."

"We've had no one but ourselves to depend on for many months," she added, wrapping her arms around her daughter. "I never thought I'd need to ask a boy—well, a young man—for assistance. But you seem like someone who can be counted on. We'll be grateful for your help."

Nick felt his face flush. Mrs. Sheridan was being kind. He wanted to tell her she was wrong—he wasn't reliable at all. She couldn't know how he'd let Gran down. Or how, just a few hours ago, he hadn't even thought to check on Annie after the earthquake.

He felt ashamed and a little scared. Nick swallowed hard and dug his fingers into his palms.

Annie lifted her head and looked at him then. Nick felt himself squirm under her gaze. It was almost as if she could see right through him.

Nick swallowed. "I'll try."

▓▓▓▓▓▓

"Just one more step, Mrs. Sheridan," Nick said as they emerged from the dim basement office onto the street. "Annie, do you have that sack of Mr. Pat's inkwells?"

"Yes, but Shake won't come," she replied. Nick could hear her talking to the dog. "Come on, boy. You can't sleep behind the sofa. Nick says we have to go."

Nick poked his head back into the dark stairway and whistled for Shake, who padded up the stairs, head down.

"He's scared," Nick said, grabbing Shake's collar. "He doesn't understand he's not safe in his own comfortable place anymore."

Finally they began to make their way down the street. Nick sniffed the air. The scent of smoke and ashes was stronger now. He couldn't even tell if the sun was still shining or not.

Nick kept his right hand under Mrs. Sheridan's elbow, trying to support her as gently as he could. But her steps were slow and uneven. Sometimes she stopped with a small gasp of pain.

Nick took a breath. In a way, he felt like they were setting off into a battlefield. Gran had told Nick about the battles his grandfather had fought in the Civil War. "The War Between the States," she'd called it.

Gran had been a bride of eighteen in 1861 when the war had begun. "Nowadays it's real common to see pictures in newspapers," she once told Nick. "But it

120

weren't always that way. I remember the first time I opened a newspaper to see a photograph of a battlefield and soldiers. Oh, I was so scared for your grandpa."

A battlefield.

At the corner, Nick turned back to look at Jackson Street. *I might not see it again,* Nick realized. He closed his eyes, trying to burn an image, make a photograph, in his memory. It was a trick he'd learned from Miss Reedy. "Use your eyes to take pictures of all you see."

Nick wanted to remember everything. Mr. Pat's store. The neat brick buildings lining the cobblestones. *It really is the prettiest street in the city,* Nick thought.

No, it's more than just pretty, he corrected himself, thinking of Mr. Pat. Nick struggled to find a word to describe how he felt about this little corner of the city. And then it came to him.

He'd been here just a few days, but still the word seemed to fit exactly right. *It's home.*

Without being told, Shakespeare padded along next to Annie. Sometimes he seemed to lean into her, as if she were a lamb he was afraid might lose her way.

Nick looked over at the big golden dog. "Good boy," he said. "Stay close."

Boom! A dynamite blast made them all jump.

Suddenly Shake turned and began to trot off, back toward Mr. Pat's store.

"Shakespeare, no!" Nick yelled while Annie ran to grab Shake's collar and pull him back. "Come on, boy."

"I can't carry my doll and the inkwells and pull Shake, too!" Annie complained. "Why couldn't we just stay behind with Mr. Lind?"

"Mr. Lind has work to do. He's trying to save his building," Nick told her. He'd thought about leaving the inkwells there. But what if Mr. Lind didn't succeed?

"Besides," he told Annie, "if the fire comes closer, everyone on Jackson Street might have to run fast. You and I . . . we have to be the brave ones to help Shake and your mama."

122

"Well, then maybe we should play a game."

"I don't know many games."

"A pretend game. Let's pretend we're going on a fun adventure. Where shall we go?"

Nick thought a minute. "How about the Palace Hotel?"

Annie nodded solemnly. "Why, thank you, Nicholas. I would love to go to the Palace Hotel with you for tea. Do you like my new gown?"

She flounced her old worn skirt a little. "I hope the cakes are good there today."

Nick grinned.

"If they are not to your liking, miss, we can go to the Eiffel Tower Restaurant instead," he told her. "After all, San Francisco is the Paris of the Pacific. See, we're passing it right now. I hear their sweet cakes are—"

"Simply delicious!" Annie finished.

But as they passed the restaurant, Nick and Annie fell silent. One wall of the building had collapsed, spilling bricks into the street. Nick helped Mrs. Sheridan skirt a pile of rubble and shattered glass.

"Don't let Shake walk in the glass, Annie," Nick warned.

He and Mr. Pat might have been going there tomorrow. Yes, tomorrow was Thursday. But all that was before. Before everything changed.

Annie sighed. "Let's just walk, Nick. I'm tired of this game."

Nick nodded. He didn't feel much like playing, either.

123

Union Square

"Sorry about this hill, ma'am," Nick said, holding on to Mrs. Sheridan's elbow.

He was trying to avoid the steepest streets on their way to Union Square. It wasn't easy, though. Nick had been surprised at that right away. It was hard to avoid walking up and down hills in San Francisco.

"I'm fine, Nick," Annie's mother assured him a little breathlessly. "I only wish I could walk faster."

Nick glanced at the smoke-filled sky. Earlier, he remembered, there had been smoke rising from different parts of the city. But now the whole sky seemed covered with black plumes.

"I can't tell what direction the fire is coming from," he said. "It's almost as if the earthquake caused a lot of small fires that are joining together to make bigger ones."

"You may be right, Nick," Mrs. Sheridan said. "I'm sure someone at Union Square can help us find out what to do."

Annie coughed. She had been trudging silently for several blocks now, holding the sack of inkwells, with her doll propped on top. She had refused to let her mother carry the small photograph of her father, and had put it in the pocket of her dress. Nick noticed her eyes seemed dark, as if the smoke and dust had blotted out their astonishing colors.

"Look at that trunk. I've been counting trunks," Annie said suddenly. "That's the fifth one I've seen in just four blocks. I want to know what happened to the people."

125

"The trunks probably just got too heavy for them," Nick offered. He thought of Tommy, struggling to pull his father's heavy trunk up these steep hills. Nick wondered what had been inside. Clothes? Letters from Tommy's mother in China?

"The people who left the trunks didn't die, did they, Nick? Do you think the fire got them? Or walls of buildings fell down on them?"

"Annie!" her mother reprimanded. "You need to be cheerful for Shakespeare's sake. Dogs can feel it when we're frightened."

"I'm sorry, Mama," Annie said quietly.

But Nick knew she wouldn't stop thinking about it.

He couldn't, either. How many people *had* died when their houses and apartments collapsed and fell? How many had been trapped by fires?

If I'd been killed in the earthquake while I was sleeping in the alley, no one would ever have missed me, Nick realized.

He glanced over at Mrs. Sheridan. Her face was pale; her lips were pressed close together. She and Annie could have been killed in the earthquake, too. Annie's father, if he ever did return, would have searched and searched but would never have found them.

"Let's go," Nick urged. "We've got to keep going."

"It's too crowded," Annie said crossly as they stood on the edge of Union Square. "Where can we sit?"

"I don't know, but let's find a place soon," her mother said, breathing heavily. "My side is throbbing."

Nick scanned the wide square, searching for an empty spot. "Let's go near the statue in the center. We'll have a good view of downtown from there."

Slowly they picked their way through the crowd. Some people had already spread blankets on the grass, as if they meant to stay the night. Others stood quietly beside toy wagons filled with pots and pans or baby buggies piled with household goods. Almost everyone, Nick noticed, faced downtown, toward Market Street, watching the fire's slow, steady progress.

Annie's mother sank onto an abandoned trunk with

a heavy sigh. "Let's hope we'll be safe for the night here. I don't believe I can take another step."

Annie nestled beside her and patted her hand. Shakespeare planted himself on Annie's feet and put his head in her lap.

Nick offered Mrs. Sheridan a drink of water from the jug. Annie pointed upward. "Nick, did you know that the lady on top of that tall marble column is called Victoria?"

Mrs. Sheridan smiled, almost for the first time. "Actually, Little Big Eyes, the statue is called Victory, not Victoria. It commemorates a victorious battle in the Spanish-American War."

"Oh, I remember you told me about that war," Annie said. "It began in 1898, the year I was born. I don't much like that I was born in the same year as a war, but at least it was a very short war. Isn't that right, Mama?"

"Yes, only a few months. But don't go on so, Annie. I expect Nicholas doesn't care about the Spanish-American War at this moment," Mrs. Sheridan said. "Except we hope this statue will bring good luck—and victory over the fire."

Nick turned away and scanned the crowd. All at once, a feeling of panic swept over him. He was just a kid from the fields. He didn't know as much as an eight-year-old. And he especially didn't know what to do next.

Mrs. Sheridan shouldn't count on him. He wasn't the right one to lead them out of danger. He turned to face her. "I . . . I don't know. . . ."

"Don't worry, Nicholas, Annie and I will be fine right here," Mrs. Sheridan interrupted him softly. "I'm sure you'll be able to find someone to help us."

"Yes, ma'am." Nick pulled his cap down low and set off.

Nick decided to see what he could find out just by listening. Ahead, a small group was gathered around one tall man. As Nick moved closer, he could see that the man's face was streaked with soot. A cut above his left eye oozed blood.

"What happened?" Nick asked the man beside him.

"He's just come from the Palace Hotel."

"All the clerks and bellboys were out on the fire escapes with hoses," Nick heard the man say. "Fires were coming our way from two directions, west and south, so we tried to soak those sides of the hotel. The heat was something awful."

Someone handed the man a jug of water. He paused and threw his head back to gulp it.

Nick pushed closer. "Did you save it?"

The man drew his hand across his eyes. "For a while I thought we could. But then the city fire department tapped the hydrant in front of the hotel—for another fire. That took our last hope. And when another building nearby on Jessie Street went up in flames . . ."

"The whole downtown will be gone by tomorrow," another man said. "The Hearst Building at Third and Market started blazing at noon. The Call Building's on fire now, too."

Nick turned away. At this rate, how long would it take the fire to reach Union Square?

Nick made for a man who stood on the corner with a horse and small cart. "Excuse me, sir, but I'm trying to get a sick woman and her child to safety. Could you take them?"

"Got a hundred bucks?" the man asked, pushing back the cap on his head.

129

"A hundred dollars?" Nick glanced to where Annie and her mother sat. Mr. Pat's inkwells in the bag at Annie's feet were surely worth more than that. Maybe this man would take them in exchange for a ride. But no. Nick couldn't do that. The inkwells belonged to Mr. Pat. And Nick had promised to keep his treasures safe.

"Don't have a cent, do you, kid? I'm sorry to hear it. Disaster like this, it's the poor who suffer the most. Just like this morning at the Valencia Street Hotel." The man turned away, spat, and then shook his head. "Crushed or burned, that's how they'll write this one in the history books."

Nick tried again. "But if you give this lady a ride, you'll be helping someone to survive."

"Wish I could, kid. But I gotta look out for myself, don't I?" The man's voice was flat, his face rigid and stern. "Otherwise it'll be me and mine under the rubble or burned to ashes in one of those tenements south of the Slot."

Nick walked quickly away. He clenched his fists and jammed them into his pockets. And then he felt the single coin still left there. He had carried it a long time. It seemed like so much and yet so little all at the same time.

130

Nick let out a long breath. He knew it was pointless to be angry at the man with the wagon. Nick had known folks just as hard. Mr. Hank. Even, sometimes, Pa.

There was that time when Nick was seven. He'd been pulling up cotton stalks when one hit his right eye. Nick remembered how he'd screamed in pain. His eye had filled with blood and he'd run back to the shack, crying.

"John, we should take this boy to the doctor," Gran had said to Pa that night as they sat eating beans. She'd washed out Nick's eye and bandaged it, but it still throbbed.

Pa finished chewing. "You doctored him fine, looks like."

"It's his eye," Gran countered. "We can't take a chance on the boy's eye."

Nick could remember sitting there, waiting for Pa's answer. But it never came. His father had simply shrugged, picked up his coffee mug, and drained it dry.

Nick stood alone, unsure what to do next. Suddenly he spotted a face he recognized.

He crept closer to get a better view, making sure to keep out of plain sight. Yes, there was that great bear of a police officer, the one who'd chased him all the way to Chinatown. Bushy Brows was standing right in the middle of Union Square, talking to a family, his hands waving here and there.

Nick bit his lip. The man might be able to help. But could he take a chance and ask? The policeman wouldn't remember him, not with all the chaos and confusion of the earthquake and fire. Or would he?

131

Nick glanced down at his clothes. Well, even with the soot and dirt, at least his shirt and pants were new. Not his hat, though. Gran had gotten it for him for his birthday last year, just before Mr. Greene had evicted them from their sharecropper's shack.

Mr. Pat had offered to buy him a new one the day they went shopping, but Nick had hesitated. "This one is good enough."

"Sentimental value, eh? I don't suppose you want to tell me about it. Well, all in good time. By all means, keep your cap. Though I do believe with that mop of yours, you'll need a cut soon."

"A cut?"

"We'll have to see how things go, but if all is well upon my return, I would certainly say a haircut is in order," Mr. Pat had told him. "I myself go to a very good barber on the edge of Chinatown, whom I highly recommend."

If all is well . . . But there would be no haircuts in Chinatown for a long time. If it wasn't already destroyed, Chinatown would soon be gone.

Nick felt a tug on his shirt.

"Nick, who are you hiding from?" Annie stood with her hands on her hips.

"I . . . I'm not . . . ," sputtered Nick.

Annie stood on tiptoes. "I know. I bet it's that policeman! I had a feeling deep inside that you were a crook, Nicholas Dray," she went on, sounding more like her old self. "Even though you were brave enough to fetch Daddy's picture and my doll. Did you steal a silver spoon from the Palace Hotel?"

"No! I never even saw the inside of the Palace." Nick stooped to tie his shoe.

"Well, then, what? I can tell you don't want him to see you," Annie said. She fingered the bump on her forehead gingerly. "Maybe Mama and I shouldn't trust you."

Trust. Well, Nick thought, why should she trust him?

He certainly hadn't been a good friend right after the earthquake. If Annie had been knocked unconscious for much longer, she and her mother might have been trapped in that building.

"Annie, I didn't do anything," Nick protested. "Bushy Brows over there thought I stole an orange and chased me. I had to run. I didn't want to get sent back to an orphanage. I hated it there."

Annie frowned. "And?"

"And what?"

"And did you take the orange?"

Nick hesitated. He wasn't sure why it mattered so much, but he wanted her to believe him. "No, not that time. But . . . but getting here from Texas, when I was on my own . . . sometimes I did steal oranges or whatever I could get."

Annie waved her hand as if the other oranges didn't matter. "If you were innocent, you have nothing to fear. Ask him for help now."

Nick hesitated. He took off his cap to scratch his head.

"You're afraid," Annie announced.

Before Nick could stick his cap back on, she'd grabbed his hand and, pulling hard, dragged him to stand before the policeman.

"Excuse me, Officer Bushy Brows," she announced in a loud voice, "we came to ask for help."

The officer's giant red brows looked wilder than ever. His face was streaked with sweat. In one hand, he held the same black club he'd pointed at Nick.

"Bushy Brows, eh?" he repeated. He looked at Nick and narrowed his eyes. "Wait a minute, I remember that head of hair. You're that thief who got away from me the other day." He paused for a moment and glanced out over the city. "The other day! Seems a lifetime ago."

"Nick didn't take that orange, sir. He has given me his word on it," Annie declared. She stepped closer to the officer and fixed him with her large bright eyes. "Nick's a hero, actually. He saved Mama and me this morning. So you have to help us."

Bushy Brows stared back at Annie. He cocked his head, as if trying to figure out what was different about her eyes. "Help you? Little girl, even if I wanted to, I can't help anyone right now."

Nick cleared his throat. "Sir, Annie's mother can't walk very well. She . . . she's expecting a baby, and she's injured. We need a wagon or an ambulance."

Bushy Brows shook his head. "I haven't seen a horse-drawn ambulance for hours. Folks with carts are asking a hundred dollars or more to haul a load. Everyone's walking."

Nick glanced toward downtown. "Do you think we'll be safe here for the night?"

"I wouldn't count on it." Bushy Brows knitted his

eyebrows together. "If I were you, I'd head across Van Ness Avenue to Golden Gate Park."

"How far to Golden Gate Park?"

The police officer shrugged. "I dunno. Maybe two, three miles."

"Three miles." Nick's heart sank. "Isn't there anything closer?"

"You might be fine on Nob Hill for the night, but I can't guarantee it." Bushy Brows pointed to a large building nearby. "See that? The St. Francis Hotel there is twelve stories. One of my buddies in the fire department tells me it'll be gutted by morning."

He turned away to answer another question. Nick and Annie stared at each other.

135

"That's our answer, then," Nick said. "But I don't think your mother can walk all night to Golden Gate Park. So let's go to Nob Hill now and hope we'll be safe there until morning."

As they set out across the square, they heard the police officer call out, "Hey, kid. Here's a warning for you: don't steal anything else. The soldiers patrolling the streets have orders to shoot looters."

"I didn't . . . ," Nick began. Then he stopped. It was pointless to argue. "All right, I won't. Thank you, sir."

Mrs. Sheridan nodded grimly when Nick told her what they'd discovered. He helped her up and then called to Shakespeare.

"Time to go, Shake." Nick reached down to pat the dog's silky back. "Hullo, you're trembling. It's all right, boy."

Shakespeare got to his feet but whined, his tail wagging weakly. Nick knelt beside him and spoke into one soft, floppy ear. Shake buried his tawny muzzle in Nick's shirt. "I know. It's smoky and loud and getting dark. And we keep getting farther and farther away from home."

Shake lifted his head and licked Nick's cheek. "You gotta trust me now, boy," Nick said softly. "We can't stay here. We have to keep moving."

MARCH OF THE FLAMES

"Annie, be careful with the bag of inkwells. Don't let them touch the sidewalk or the glass ones will break," Nick warned. "Do you want me to carry it?"

"No, I'm strong enough! It's just so steep on this hill. It's like we're walking straight up into the air," Annie panted. "Are you all right, Mama?"

Annie's mother stopped and nodded, too winded to speak.

They kept on, moving slowly, one step at a time. Once in a while, Nick could hear Annie's mother catch her breath in pain. But he didn't see her cry as she struggled up the steep streets. It was only later, as they huddled in the empty doorway of a Nob Hill mansion on California Street, that he noticed her tear-streaked face.

"I'm so sorry, ma'am. It must hurt a lot." Nick wished that the door would open and someone would invite them in to spend the night on a real bed. But the house was dark.

Mrs. Sheridan rested her back against a tall white column and shook her head. "It's not only that. I just can't believe the city is being destroyed like this. So many people . . . losing loved ones, homes, businesses, everything they have."

"We lost our home, too, Mama," said Annie. Nick watched her peel one of Tommy's oranges. Had Tommy been able to drag his trunk up steep Nob Hill? Nick had kept watch for his friend all day. But he didn't really expect to find him in all the confusion and chaos.

138

"Yes, we lost our home, but we have each other, Little Big Eyes," Annie's mother said softly, reaching over to brush away some ashes that clung to Annie's hair.

"And Daddy, and my new brother or sister," Annie reminded her. "Someday, maybe we'll all live together in a house like this one."

Annie looked up at the dark windows. "I bet they have a piano, and real china dishes, and beautiful woven rugs, all gold and red." She pointed to the bag of inkwells at her feet. "I wonder if the gentleman and the lady each has a desk to write letters on, with one of Mr. Pat's pretty inkwells on it."

"It looks like the owners have already left to go someplace safe," said Nick, patting Shakespeare to keep him from trembling. Shake had seemed more nervous the farther away they got from Jackson Street. "I'd fight to save this house if it was mine. I wouldn't leave it."

"Well, Nick, I believe you would leave if you had to. But perhaps the fire won't march this far. Maybe it will spare Nob Hill's beautiful homes." Mrs. Sheridan closed her eyes.

But what will stop it? Nick couldn't help thinking. The firemen didn't have the water they needed. And the dynamite didn't seem to be working, either.

Shake pushed his nose into Nick's lap. "You want scratches, do you, boy? You're still trembling a little. It will be all right."

Shake wagged his tail weakly. He got to his feet, his nails clicking on the stone steps.

"No, don't go anywhere, Shake. We're staying here tonight. Come settle down," Nick called him back. It took a long time before Shake heaved himself down beside Nick with a long sigh.

Nick fought hard to stay awake and keep watch. Try as he might, he couldn't keep his eyes open. Sometime later, in the middle of the night, Nick thought he heard shouts. He might have been dreaming; he couldn't be sure. But later he remembered hearing the words "Union Square. St. Francis Hotel."

When Nick did wake up, it took him a long time to realize where he was. A strange red glow lit the sky. He squinted. Was that the sun? For a moment he half expected to hear Gran's voice. *Daybreak, Nicholas. Time to pick.*

But then the ash and smoke in the air made him cough. Gray curtains of smoke blotted out the small red sun. Nick rubbed his eyes, still heavy with sleep. He felt bruised and sore and a little confused. Maybe that's why it took him a few minutes to notice what he should have seen right away.

They were in worse danger than ever. The fire hadn't stopped in the night but had kept on, devouring one building after another. Nick remembered the voices he'd heard. Probably they were real. The fire must have swept over Union Square and attacked the St. Francis Hotel. Now it was creeping up to attack the mansions on Nob Hill.

"It's chasing us the way Bushy Brows chased me," Nick said to himself. Even from where he sat, he could see red glowing flames licking at the roof of a three-story mansion a block away. Soldiers began to shout at other people huddled in doorways to get moving before the march of the fire.

Nick shivered and rubbed his hip. The stone step was cold and uncomfortable. All night he'd felt the warmth of the big golden dog curled beside him. But now his side felt chilled.

And that's when it hit him: Shakespeare wasn't there.

Nick jumped to his feet, scrambled off the steps,

and scanned the street in all directions. Shakespeare wasn't in sight. And suddenly Nick guessed what had happened.

Shake must have gotten scared in the night. And he'd headed straight for home.

Mr. Pat had said that Shake knew his way from just about anywhere in the city. Probably, Nick thought, Shake had been in this neighborhood before with Mr. Pat. Nick imagined Mr. Pat and his "faithful canine companion" delivering a crystal inkwell to a rich lady in one of these mansions—maybe the one that was burning right now. Yes, Shakespeare would know how to get home.

But not now. How could Shake get home now? Not on these streets, blackened by flames or barricaded by rubble. Not with firemen blasting dynamite. Not with soldiers patrolling with loaded rifles.

Nick looked at the approaching fire, then back at the stone steps. Annie was still asleep, curled up against her mother, the bag of inkwells beside her. If he could just get back down to Jackson Street, he might have time to find Shakespeare and bring him back.

Nick saw two soldiers coming toward him and his heart sank. There was no time. The fire was coming. And it was coming fast.

141

CHASED BY FIRE

"Hey, kid. Time to move!" a soldier shouted at Nick.

Nick had an idea. Maybe the soldiers could take charge of Annie and her mother. He'd be able to slip away and find Shake. "Sir. I have a woman here who can't walk very well. Can you get us an ambulance or a cart?"

"Too late for that. You should have left this part of the city yesterday," the soldier said shortly. "Most of the downtown is in ruins. Today the fire will be eating its way through these houses."

The other soldier gestured down the street. "You got about fifteen minutes before the fire reaches this block, kid. Less if the wind changes direction. Move along now."

Nick felt a hand on his shoulder. It was Annie's mother, looking disheveled and pale. She was staring down the block, her eyes wide. "My goodness, I can see fire licking at the curtains of that grand house. I can't bear to think of all those fine things inside!"

Gran would have liked Mrs. Sheridan, Nick thought. She wasn't at all jealous of the rich people who lived on Nob Hill, only sad for their losses.

Nick turned his back on the fire. He didn't want to think of Shake trying to find his way back to Jackson Street. He made himself concentrate on what he had to do. He went back to the stoop and picked up the water jug. There were only two oranges left, so he stuck one in each jacket pocket.

Annie was on the sidewalk. She was staring at the house, too. "Mama, look! I can see red pricks of flame on the roof. And you can hear the crackling from here."

143

"Now, Annie. We have to go now," Nick urged, taking hold of Mrs. Sheridan's arm. "We don't have time to look at it. Come on."

He walked a few steps, hoping she'd follow. But Annie was rooted in the middle of the sidewalk. "Wait, Nick. Shakespeare! Where's Shake?"

Nick swallowed hard and stared at the ground. "Shake is gone. When I woke up this morning, he wasn't here."

He didn't dare look at Annie. He heard her gasp. "But the fire's coming. We can't leave him."

Nick went back to her and grabbed her hand. "We have to go. Come on. We have to help your mother. We can't wait. The fire's chasing us and it's not going to stop."

"But, Nick . . . you can't leave poor Shake. He'll be scared. He could be hiding anywhere." Annie's voice trembled.

Nick didn't let go of her hand. "Shake isn't here, Annie. I'm sure he went home, back to Jackson Street."

Annie jerked her hand away. She planted her feet. "How could you let him run away? Why didn't you hold on to him last night?"

"Annie, start walking now," Mrs. Sheridan ordered in the fiercest voice Nick had heard her use. "It's not Nick's fault. Don't you see he wants to go after his dog? But we can't. There's no time."

144

Annie stood for a minute, her eyes brimming with tears. Then she flew to her mother's right side and began to walk. Nick saw that her face was set and her shoulders trembled. They kept to the middle of the street, straggling behind other people who were, like them, fleeing before the great heat and greedy flames.

Annie was right, Nick thought. He'd been stupid. He should never have slept. If only he'd stayed awake, he could have kept Shake from running away. He could have gotten them up and moving sooner. Instead, he'd put them in danger. And he'd lost Shake. How could he ever tell Mr. Pat?

Whoosh! Crack!

Nick whirled around, startled. Annie screamed.

Down the street, the house that had been slowly burning had suddenly erupted into flames. Nick felt as if he was staring into the mouth of a furnace. Red crackling tongues of fire leaped into the air. Enormous waves of smoke rolled out of the house and spewed into the sky, darker than any storm cloud. Nick felt a rush of intense heat push over him.

There was no air. They would be smothered.

"Run. We have to run!" Nick tried to shout. But his voice came out a hoarse whisper.

Nick hurried them along as fast as Annie's mother could walk. Every few steps, he turned to look over his shoulder. Each time it seemed to him the roar of the fire was louder. Firemen, soldiers, and frightened people swarmed the street.

At the corner, they passed more soldiers with rifles. "Keep moving. The fire's not far behind."

"We know," Nick said crossly. "We're doing the best we can."

He felt angry and worried about Shake. He tried not to imagine Shake padding along, his tongue lolling, trying to find his way home.

Annie's mother stopped to catch her breath. She held her side. "It hurts to talk, Nicholas," she whispered. "Please ask them about the park."

Nick nodded. "Sir, is this the way to Golden Gate Park? Will we be safe there?"

"You will if we can hold the fire at Van Ness Avenue. The firemen are starting to dynamite every building between here and Van Ness to try to make a break. Van Ness is wide, and it's our last chance to save the rest of the city," the soldier told him.

"You're on California Street now. Just keep on this way until you get past Van Ness Avenue, ma'am." The other soldier addressed Mrs. Sheridan. "The park is a ways past there, but someone will be able to direct you. There should be tents set up at Golden Gate Park already. The army is serving rations, and there's a makeshift hospital."

146

"Have you seen a big golden dog?" Annie piped up suddenly.

The soldiers didn't answer her. They had already turned away to talk to an old man dragging a trunk.

"I'm not leaving it behind," Nick heard the man say. "No matter what!"

"I don't like those soldiers," Annie complained as they walked away. "Especially their rifles."

"I believe they've been sent to keep order and stop looting," her mother explained in a soft voice. "It's best to stay out of their way."

"They better not shoot Shakespeare," Annie said.

"Annie!" her mother scolded in a hoarse whisper. "Don't say such things. Can't you see Nick is upset enough about his dog?"

"Shake isn't even Nick's dog," said Annie. "He belongs to Mr. Pat."

She passed an abandoned trunk and kicked at it with her foot. She kicked so hard that she dropped the cloth doll in her hand.

Nick stopped and watched her stoop to pick it up. His stomach felt queasy. "Annie, where's the bag? The bag with Mr. Pat's inkwells?"

"I must have forgot it back on the steps," she said. He looked at her face.

"Oh, Annie, Annie Sheridan! You forgot it on purpose, didn't you?" Mrs. Sheridan's eyes widened. "That's a horrible thing. After everything Nick has done for us. It wasn't his fault—he didn't mean to let the dog go. Oh, Nick. I'm so sorry."

Annie stared at the ground and began to walk without a word.

Nick stood still, too angry to speak. He felt like screaming at her, but no words came out. He wanted to cry. But he'd never cried much. He hadn't even cried for Gran. Instead the tears seemed stuck inside, the way cotton seeds stick to fiber in the boll.

He let out a breath and swallowed hard. In a way, he could see why Annie had done that to get back at him.

Mr. Pat had trusted him to take care of Shake. And he had failed.

147

ACROSS VAN NESS

𐍈𐍈𐍈𐍈

Boom! The sounds of dynamite rang in their ears,
closer and closer.

"The air feels so hot," Annie complained once. But
mostly she was silent and sulky.

It was hard to walk. The street was crowded with
soldiers, firemen, and people fleeing their homes. Nick
was worried someone would push past Mrs. Sheridan and cause her more pain. Annie stayed by her
mother's other side now, as far away from Nick as she
could get.

"Oh, I'm sorry," Mrs. Sheridan gasped as she
paused to rest on a corner. She held one hand over her
waist. "I . . . I simply can't go any faster."

"The baby, Mama?" Annie whispered.

"No, Annie. Not quite yet. But I'm nearly done in,
I'm afraid," her mother replied. She looked at Nick.
"How much farther?"

"I don't really know. But we've been walking so long, I think we must be close to Van Ness."

Nick hoped he was right. The truth was, he felt like he was in a dream, running through a dark, smoky haze. No matter how hard he tried, he could move only inches at a time. It was like trying to run on the bottom of a pond.

A family of three passed them. The man dragged a trunk, and his wife carried two enormous paintings in gilded frames. Beside them was a little boy holding a squirmy puppy in his arms.

"Oh, there's that awful sound again of trunks scraping along the streets. I believe I heard it all night long, or perhaps it was just my dreams," Annie's mother exclaimed. "Did you hear it, Annie?"

Annie shook her head. She wasn't thinking about trunks. She had been watching the boy with the puppy.

Annie poked her head around her mother and stared across at Nick with accusing eyes. He wanted to yell at her to leave him alone.

"This must be Van Ness."

They had reached a wide street. Across it, on the west side, crowds of people stood, carrying baskets, suitcases, and satchels. Nick saw two men trying to push a piano down the street.

"We should be safe here for a little while, at least. You can rest on the stone steps of that building, Mrs.

Sheridan." Nick pointed. Mrs. Sheridan lowered herself slowly onto the steps.

"I don't see any tents here," said Annie, pouting. "I thought we were going to the park."

A woman beside them in a white blouse and dark blue skirt leaned over. "Golden Gate Park is still blocks away, dearie."

Annie's mother sighed and dropped her face in her hands.

The woman reached over and patted Mrs. Sheridan on her shoulder. "There, there. You look all done in. I was just about to open my basket and have some bread and cheese. There's enough for you and your children."

"He's not my brother," Annie said under her breath, but loud enough for Nick to hear.

Nick bit his tongue. Jumping to his feet, he pulled the last two oranges out of his pockets. He handed them to Mrs. Sheridan. "Here, eat these, too. I'll look around and see what I can find out."

Before long, Nick was back. "We can't stay here. The dynamite is making the fire worse in some places," he told Mrs. Sheridan. "Folks are afraid that the fire will leap Van Ness and begin burning this side of the street."

"So we're not safe even now?"

Nick shook his head. "I heard someone say the firemen may try to run a hose to the bay all the way along Van Ness Avenue to Sacramento Street. That's only one block away from here. They say they have to stop it now or the whole western part of the city will burn."

For a minute Nick thought she would cry. But then Annie's mother held out her hand. "Please help me up, then, Nicholas. This fire has chased us all day, but we can't give up now. Annie, are you ready?"

Annie looked back toward where they had come from. Her lips were pressed close together. The bump on her forehead had shrunk, but it looked as red as ever.

Nick could almost see what she was thinking. Every step took them farther away from Shake and from the house where Annie hoped her father would come looking for her.

'151

"Now, Annie," her mother commanded.

We don't have a choice, Nick thought. *The fire won't give us one.*

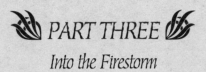

PART THREE

Into the Firestorm

Oh! The terrors of the night!

All around us was one roaring,

crackling furnace of flames.

—Rose M. Quinn, survivor

THURSDAY NIGHT

The rest of the day passed in a blur. It was almost dark when they reached Golden Gate Park. Long rows of white tents already dotted the open spaces.

They stood in line for rations, and then Nick found a Red Cross volunteer, who directed them to a large tent where a makeshift hospital had been set up.

"Oh, I am so thankful to be here. Can my daughter stay with me?" Annie's mother asked the nurse as she sank down gratefully on a cot.

"Is your husband not with you?"

"My father is coming later," Annie put in before Mrs. Sheridan could answer.

"Well, then, both your children can stay if you like, if they don't mind blankets on the ground," the nurse said.

155

Annie shot Nick a glance but clamped her lips together and kept silent.

Long after Annie and her mother had fallen asleep,
Nick lay on his blanket tossing and turning. He should
have been exhausted, but sleep wouldn't come.

It had been dark for hours when Nick reached for
his shoes and, holding them in one hand, tiptoed softly
between the rows of cots. Outside the tent, he sat on
the ground to put them on.

He heard a rustle behind him.

"What are you doing?"

"Go back to sleep, Annie." Nick tied his other shoe.

She hissed softly, "You're going to find Shake, aren't
you?"

Nick got to his feet and stood looking at her silently.

"It's not safe," she whispered.

"I would have gone back this morning if I could
have."

Annie hung her head. "I know. Nick . . . I'm
sorry . . . about the inkwells. And for being mean."

"That's not why I'm going." Nick pulled his cap
down low. "He was *my* responsibility. I promised Mr.
Pat I'd take care of him. Shake doesn't understand
what's happening. He misses Mr. Pat; he just wanted
to go home. Besides, Shake . . ."

He faltered.

"I love Shake, too," Annie said after a minute. She

peered up at him. "Well, since you *will* go, can I come?"

"No, you can't. What would your mama do then?"

"But . . . but we won't ever see you again. You don't care about us." Annie sniffled. "Especially after today."

Nick sighed. They stood in the darkness.

At last he said, "That's not true, Annie. We're friends, no matter what. I . . . I don't have many friends."

Annie pulled at one of her braids. "I don't, either. Just Mama and Daddy. And I don't even know if he . . ."

Annie turned her face up at him. "How will I know?"

"Know what?"

"Know that you'll come back and find us?"

"Oh, you want a guarantee." Nick thought a minute. He reached into his pocket and drew out his other coin.

"Keep this for me a little while, will you, Annie Sheridan?" He handed it to her. "I'll come back and get it."

"What is it?"

Nick let out his breath. "It looks just like any other coin, but it's not. It's special. It's something I remember my gran by."

"Like the picture of my father." Annie closed her

157

fist tight around it. "I'll keep it safe till you come back."

Nick took a few steps, then turned. "Do you still fly to the North Star to help your father find his way?"

Annie nodded wordlessly.

"Well, I'd sure like it if you did that for me tonight, Annie of the North Star."

For the first time, Annie smiled. "I will. I can do that."

Nick made good time on the streets between Golden Gate Park and Van Ness Avenue. But he knew the hardest part lay ahead. Somehow, he would have to get back to Jackson Street. It would have been difficult in daylight, but the darkened city seemed like an eerie, smoky battlefield.

"Did the fire jump Van Ness?" Nick asked the first man he met.

"In a few places," came the answer. "But the firemen made their stand there. Put a hose all the way down Van Ness to the bay. And they beat it down with wet blankets, too. Thank goodness they've stopped it."

Nick's spirits lifted. "So the fire is completely out?"

"Oh, no! Not everywhere, at least. There are still fires blazing on the other side of Van Ness." The man turned and pointed back toward Market Street. "From what I hear, every time the wind blows, the fire turns back on itself and destroys blocks folks thought had been spared."

Nick thanked him and set off again. At least Annie and her mother would have nothing to worry about now. Golden Gate Park would be safe. But the man's news worried him, too. The fire was not yet out. And places that had been safe, like Jackson Street, might still be in danger.

At every step, Nick imagined Shakespeare making his way back, snaking around the paths of the fire, trembling when the dynamite exploded. One frightened dog, determined to go home. But what if he hadn't been able to make it?

159

Nick scurried faster. This journey seemed to be taking a long time—too long. It wasn't just avoiding the horrible fingers of flame. He had to pick his way over piles of rubble and skirt deep fissures that had buckled the cobblestones. Some streets were completely impassable. Firemen had blockaded others. Explosions rang out, and Nick thought of his grandfather on the battlefield. Maybe, he thought, it had felt a little like this.

And then there were the soldiers. In a strange way, the soldiers with their long rifles frightened Nick most of all. He swallowed hard. If the soldiers found him, they wouldn't let him near Jackson Street. He had to stay out of their way. He didn't want to think what they'd do if they thought he was a looter.

Nick quickened his steps and kept on.

It seemed hours since he'd left Annie. It must be after midnight—already Friday. Wednesday, Thursday, and now Friday. Three days of destruction and fire. More than anything, he wished it would end.

He was getting closer. Turning a corner, Nick found himself alone on a deserted street, surrounded by the skeletal ruins of gutted buildings. The city had become a strange, menacing place, unlike anywhere he'd ever been. The smoldering beams and walls emitted odd crackling noises. Ashes floated through the air. He could feel waves of heat from the force of the flames.

Crack! Nick jumped. One wall, all that was left of a blackened one-story house, suddenly tumbled onto the sidewalk behind him.

I'm not sure I can do this, Nick thought with a shiver.

And then he heard footsteps.

For a moment, Nick panicked. He stood frozen, unable to move. Where could he hide?

There. An alley. Nick raced into a narrow street and crouched down behind a pile of timber and bricks. He tried not to breathe. At least he had heard the footsteps first. He was getting back to being Nick the Invisible—instead of being caught off guard by big lumbering policemen like Bushy Brows.

Nick peered through the dark haze. The two approaching men weren't soldiers after all. Instead two police officers passed, carrying what looked like a corpse.

INTO THE FIRESTORM

After what seemed like hours of wrong turns, Nick began to recognize his neighborhood. He was almost to Jackson Street.

He couldn't see any fire, but all at once the smoke was thicker. He had to cover his eyes to keep live embers from hitting them.

Nick raced the rest of the way. He turned the corner, and there was Jackson Street.

"It's still here! Mr. Pat's store hasn't burned down," he cried.

Nick could barely make out figures running here and there through the smoke. He heard a voice yell, "The fire's hitting from the north. Pacific Street is going! There's only the alley of Gold Street separating Jackson Street from the flames now."

I'm in time, just in time, Nick realized. Ed Lind's plan had worked for a while. The neighborhood had made it through Wednesday and Thursday. But now the fire was doubling back, attacking from a new direction.

Nick coughed. Smoke blew everywhere. If Shakespeare had come back to Mr. Pat's store, he'd have to act fast. The building might not last much longer.

"Who's there? Stop."

The smoke was so thick, Nick heard the man before he saw him.

A tall young soldier was blocking his way. The soldier raised his rifle. "I got orders to shoot looters."

Nick swallowed hard. Out of the corner of his eye, he could see Ed Lind's whiskey warehouse across the street. Nick didn't know how many barrels of whiskey were still left inside, but if the fire reached them, the whole block would be engulfed in seconds.

He was afraid the soldier would grab him, pin him down. There wasn't time to explain.

Nick turned on his heel and sprang away toward the doorway of Mr. Pat's office.

Crack! It might have been a shot, or maybe it was just the sound of flames lapping at wooden beams. Nick didn't stop.

He half ran, half fell down the few steps to the little basement room. He could feel the sweat rolling in large droplets down his back and running down his forehead.

163

"Shakespeare! Where are you? Come here! Please, boy." His throat felt seared from the smoke and the flying ash.

Nick stumbled across the room to the sofa. He ran his hands along the old cushions, still calling for Shake. But he wasn't there.

One wall was smoking now, and the crackling sounds grew louder. Nick heard muffled shouts from the street. The soldier would be waiting. Or he might even come looking for him.

"Shakespeare, Shake. Are you here?"

No answer. Nick coughed. It was hard to see. He should go. And then he heard something.

"Shakespeare! Where are you, boy? It's me, Nick."

The whine came again.

Nick knelt down to search behind the sofa. He reached out, and his hand touched soft fur.

"Shake, you're here!" Nick pulled with one hand. "We were so worried. But you can't wait for Mr. Pat here, boy."

The big dog lifted his head but made no effort to move. He seemed sluggish. *The smoke,* Nick thought.

He managed to grab the dog's collar. "All right, I got you. Let's get out of this smoke."

Nick pulled. "Come on, boy."

But Shakespeare bent his head and dug his toes into the floor.

I've got to keep calm, Nick told himself. *I don't*

*want to make him any more scared than he is. There's
not much time.*

"Come on, boy," Nick coaxed again. Ten seconds,
twenty. Shake wouldn't come on his own.

"All right. If that's what we have to do. It's lucky for
you I'm strong from hauling all those bags of cotton,
Shake," he murmured softly, trying to keep his voice
calm.

Reaching under Shake, he heaved and pulled him
out from behind the sofa. Nick coughed hard. He didn't
want to carry the heavy dog. But he had no choice.

"Let's go!"

With a deep breath, Nick bent down and lifted the
trembling animal. He lurched back under Shake's weight
and almost toppled to the floor. Shakespeare made noises
deep in his throat. He struggled to get free.

"Hold on, keep still, boy. It's all right," Nick gasped.

They made their way slowly toward the stairway.
The heat pressed down on Nick. Time seemed to stand
still.

Sometimes, on the hottest afternoons in the cotton
fields, time had seemed to slow down just like this.
The pain, the heat, the sun, the same motion of picking
again and again. It had numbed him until there was
nothing left. He was only a machine—unfeeling, un-
caring, just doing a job. The real part of him shut off.
Shut off.

Maybe that's why he'd never been able to cry when

165

Pa left, or even on that last day with Gran. Instead, all the grief had pressed him down, as if he were buried under a heavy bale of cotton.

Nick coughed. The smoke and the dim light made it hard to see. How many steps were there? Nick tried to remember. Five? Six?

He'd been stupid. He hadn't understood how sick Gran really was. Maybe if he'd paid attention, he could have found help sooner, forced Mr. Hank to call a doctor. Something. It had been his fault.

And it would be his fault now, too, if he lost Shakespeare. He had to get out now, no matter what. Even if it meant the soldier waiting on the street arrested him—or worse.

One step, two steps. Then a third.

Suddenly, just as Nick caught a glimpse of the swirling smoke outside, he tripped again. He stumbled and put out one hand to keep from falling down.

Shakespeare whined, pushing against him, struggling in fear, trying hard to get free, to hide in the dark, safe place he knew.

"I won't let go of you!" Nick felt like his lungs, or maybe his heart, would burst. Nick held the big dog like an unwieldy baby. He panted and coughed again.

Don't let go, don't let go.

Nick reached the street. He stood for a second, breathing heavily, his throat sore.

Then he sank to the ground holding tight to the big

golden dog. He could feel tears streaming down his cheeks, but he didn't know when he'd begun to cry.

Nick buried his face in Shakespeare's fur. Shake was safe. But still it felt like he'd failed at so much else. He'd lost Mr. Pat's treasures and maybe Mr. Pat. He'd lost Pa.

Most of all, he'd lost Gran. His chest hurt so bad with the thought of her. He wanted the sound of her soft, familiar voice. He felt the sobs cut through him, shaking him from the inside out.

And then Nick looked up, straight into the barrel of a gun.

A GOOD DOG

A voice shouted, "You, kid."

"Wait!" Nick raised one hand in the air, keeping hold of Shake's collar with the other. He wasn't taking any chances.

"I can shoot you for this," the soldier growled. "Why'd you go back in there when I yelled at you to stop?"

Nick didn't let go of Shake. "I had to. My . . . dog was in there."

"A dog? You went back in there for a dog?"

"He's a good dog, sir. A very good dog," Nick cried hoarsely. He wanted to rub the sweat and tears and soot from his face, but he didn't dare let go.

"He certainly is a good dog," said another voice, though Nick couldn't see who it was in the smoke.

Shakespeare broke free of Nick's arm with a force that sent Nick flat on his back, his cap sprawling.

"I'd appreciate it if you would kindly stop pointing that distasteful weapon at my apprentice here, soldier," the voice continued, struggling to talk from behind a barking, leaping bundle of fur. "Don't you have better things to do than to threaten young heroes, especially in the midst of a raging fire?"

"Mr. Pat!" Nick gulped, and the tears started again.

The soldier stepped back as Mr. Pat rushed over and pulled Nick to his feet. "No time for that now. I've just arrived. I thought all was lost. But you're safe, thank God."

"But . . . your store . . . your treasures," croaked Nick in a whisper.

"Sorry, sir. Didn't know he belonged to you," the soldier said, his rifle lowered now. "The boy defied my orders."

"Pat! Come on," someone yelled. Nick saw Ed Lind and some soldiers stampeding toward them.

"The wind's turned suddenly. We think we might have one last chance to save Jackson Street," Ed yelled. "We don't have water. But I've got a wine pump from the wine merchant on Washington Street. We're going to tap into a manhole and use sewage to fight the fire."

"Sewage?" asked Mr. Pat, turning up his nose.

"Yes, sewage! We're going to make a bucket brigade of sewage."

Nick scrambled to his feet and wiped his face with a corner of his shirt. "I'll help, too."

169

▐▌▐▌▐▌

The bucket brigade was in full force, but at first Nick felt sure it was too late. Flames had begun eating through the buildings on the north side of Jackson Street. Mr. Pat's building was brick, but most everything inside it—floor, ceilings, and furnishings—was made of wood. The store couldn't last long.

But the soldiers, firemen, Ed Lind, and his bucket warriors didn't let up. Before long Nick's hands were blistered and red.

"Sorry about that, kid," said the soldier who passed him the bucket. He was the same one who'd taken him for a looter.

"He really is a good dog," Nick repeated. Shakespeare was jumping to and fro near Pat's feet now, barking at the flames, the soldiers, and the smelly buckets.

"I'm glad to see you, too, boy," Pat Patterson told his dog with a laugh. "But if you don't stop barking, I'm going to dump a bucket of sewage on your head."

The smell, Nick thought, was awful. He'd never been so dirty and grimy before, even in the fields. He'd never heard of fighting a fire with sewage before. It hit the flames and the smoldering woodwork with a suffocating steam.

Shakespeare began to howl.

Mr. Pat threw back his head. "By God, this is awful stuff, Ed. You're a lunatic."

"I might be a lunatic, Pat. But I'm a smart one.

Look, we're slowing the fire down. It's not going to get past those buildings after all."

They were making a last stand. The buildings on the corners had collapsed, including Annie's rooming house. But with the wet sewage to protect the buildings and wind blowing the fire back into itself, the flames on Jackson Street slowly began to die down.

"We're doing it. Don't let up. Keep it from coming closer!" Ed Lind urged the bucket brigade workers on.

Nick fought to keep up, passing one bucket after another along the line. His palms hurt from holding the heavy buckets, but he didn't care. He was helping to save Jackson Street.

171

"Look over there. I can't see any red flickers anymore, just puffs of smoke," Nick called out to Mr. Pat.

"I think you're right, my boy. We may save our home yet."

An hour later, they had doused the last flickering tongue of fire. Puffs of smoke still rose from the cinders. But the smoke had already begun to clear.

Ed Lind led the cheer, tossing his bucket into the air. "Hurrah! We've stopped it! Jackson Street is saved."

The men cheered and clapped one another on the back. They laughed at their slimy, filthy clothes.

"What a motley crew this is," Ed Lind crowed, smiling through the soot that covered his face. "Just look at us—firemen, policemen, soldiers, clerks, and whiskey barrel rollers. Good job, all!"

"And here's a reporter, too," Mr. Pat said, pointing to a man standing nearby. "I say, James, my friend, I've got a story for your paper. This orphan boy here has been in my employ for only a few days, but he risked his life—and this soldier's gunfire—to rescue my dog. Write it up for your readers and show them that the spirit of San Francisco isn't dead yet, though the entire city is lost."

The reporter took out his notebook and began to scribble. "Just the sort of story folks want to read—'Boy Hero Risks All to Save Dog.'"

Not a hero, Nick thought. *Just an ordinary San Francisco kid.*

172

PART FOUR
San Francisco Spirit

There is no water, and still less soap.

We have no city, but lots of hope.

—Anonymous inscription
scribbled on the ruins of Market
Street after the fire

What Matters

Nick, Ed, Mr. Pat, and Shakespeare spent the night in the whiskey warehouse.

At first Nick was anxious. "How do we know for sure the fire won't come back?"

"Don't worry," said Ed, handing out rags for them to wipe their arms and faces with. "I've got guards posted over the whiskey barrels and the street. If there's any danger, and I don't think there will be, they'll wake us up."

Mr. Pat shook his head. "You're a genius, Ed. Do you know this is one of the few unburnt blocks in the city?"

"No thanks to you, Pat. Where were you all this time, anyway?" his friend asked.

"I came as quickly as I could, but I had a hard time getting back to the city. And an even harder time getting a pass," Mr. Pat explained. "What an unbelievable sight it was from across the bay. You couldn't find the words to describe it."

He was lying with his head against Shakespeare's warm side. The dog nuzzled his neck as if to apologize for being so much trouble.

Nick didn't notice. He had fallen asleep at last.

Nick awoke Saturday morning to good news. All across the city, the fires were out. The great clouds of smoke had disappeared.

Later he and Mr. Pat picked their way through the store. "Some fire damage, some earthquake damage. But the building itself survived," said Mr. Pat. "We are luckier than most. Why, almost all the downtown is gone. Hundreds of blocks destroyed."

Nick followed Mr. Pat around silently. He had to tell him. But it was hard. It wasn't until they were in the small room in the basement that Nick finally got the courage to speak.

"Mr. Pat, I . . . I collected the best inkwells and pens I could find on the first day, right after the earthquake." Nick swallowed hard. "But then, well, I . . . I lost them. I'm sorry. I didn't do a very good job."

Mr. Pat waved his hand. "You saved my favorite treasure, isn't that right, faithful canine companion?"

Shakespeare sat back on his haunches, a giant smile

lighting up his chocolate brown eyes. He was back to his old spunky self.

"But something else is lost I wish I could find," murmured Mr. Pat. He had dropped to his hands and knees and was searching the floor. "I can't seem to find that old family photograph."

"It's not here?"

Mr. Pat shook his head. "It's funny what you care about in the end, what matters most. That picture, Shake here, and . . . well, I admit I was worried sick about you."

Mr. Pat cleared his throat. "Anyway, you'll be glad to know I haven't totally forgotten the business. I brought back paper, some postcards, pencils, and pens."

Nick frowned. "Will people want paper and pens now?"

"Ah, my boy, you have a lot to learn yet. Folks will want to write letters and postcards to let their kin know they've survived the great tragedy," Mr. Pat said, waving his arms. "And that reminds me, didn't you say your penmanship was excellent?"

"Well, I can make letters. But I'm not so good at spelling."

"Few people are," Mr. Pat observed. "At any rate, I'm going to send you over to the post office with a crate to write on. For a few pennies, you can write letters for folks who can't do it themselves. I hear the post office will accept anything and isn't charging for stamps until the crisis is over. How does that sound?"

Nick hesitated. There was something he wanted to ask. He bit his lip.

"What, you don't want to work for me after all?" asked Mr. Pat, looking closely at Nick. "Well, this is temporary, let me assure you. Once the schools open up again, you're going, young man. Work will be after school and Saturdays only. We'll make a good speller out of you."

"So . . . so you want me to stay?"

"After what you did for Shakespeare and me, you can stay here as long as you want, Nicholas Dray. And that's what I told my friend, the reporter from the *Call*, too," Mr. Pat went on. "I expect we'll see that story about you any day now."

178

Mr. Pat tapped his nose. "My motives were not entirely pure, I admit. While I certainly hope your story inspires our fellow citizens, I also made sure he included where you work and that we'll be open for business. So let's get busy, shall we?"

"I . . . I do want to work, and go to school, and stay here," said Nick, the words tumbling out in a rush. "But . . . but I can't start today. At least right now."

Mr. Pat raised his eyebrows. "Ah, for a minute you had me worried. A prior engagement, perhaps?"

"It's just that I want to check on my friends."

"Friends? You have friends?" Mr. Pat looked

amused. "Why, I thought Shakespeare and I were your only friends in the world, at least as of the beginning of this eventful and unforgettable week."

Nick relaxed and grinned. He'd forgotten how much fun it was just to listen to Mr. Pat. "Well, yes and no. I met a boy named Tommy in Chinatown, but the last time I saw him, he was trying to escape the flames. He might be at the Presidio, or maybe he found a way out of the city already.

"And then there's Annie Sheridan and her mother, who lived in the rooming house on the corner. I left them in Golden Gate Park. I don't know if I can find them again, but I'd like to be sure they're safe."

"Ah, I remember, the voluble Annie." Mr. Pat nodded. He thought a moment, then reached into his pocket and handed Nick a small money purse. "There's not much in here, but please give this to Annie's mother for me. Tell her we'll do all we can to bring them back as our neighbors on Jackson Street."

"Gee, Mr. Pat, thanks." Nick started to go. After a few steps, he looked back. Shakespeare sat close to Mr. Pat, looking up at his master, wagging his tail.

Mr. Pat saw his glance. "Shakespeare, your young master has a mission, and I believe he'd like some company. You'd better go with him."

"Can I really take him?" Nick asked. "Come on, Shake."

"Go with him, Shakespeare. Nick's part of the

establishment now." Mr. Pat tapped Shake on his shoulder and the dog sprang across to Nick in a graceful bound. "Be careful. I'll see what I can do to round up something edible and commence the sad task of assessing the true damage to our business. And when you come back, let's see if we can find some water for baths—for all of us!"

Nick paused on the steps. "Mr. Pat, I just want to—"

Pat Patterson pointed a finger into the air. "Nick, if we are to be a team . . . well, one might even go so far as to say a family . . . just plain Pat will do."

180

Nick grinned. "Thanks, Pat. My grandmother—"

Nick stopped. He took his hat off and twisted it in his hands. It was black with soot and threadbare in some places. He thought of Gran pulling out her glove, putting by some money to buy him a new cap.

"My grandmother liked to laugh. She loved beautiful things, like flowers. I don't think she got much beauty in her life. But she'd be happy to know . . . to know I'm here," Nick said slowly. He struggled to find the right words. "Gran wanted . . . well, she wanted me to have the world."

Then Nick whistled. "Come on, Shake, let's go."

SHAKESPEARE'S NAMESAKES

The swirling winds and the smoke of the firestorms were gone. An eerie quiet lay over the city streets, or what was left of them. It was daylight now, not night. And as Nick picked his way carefully around bricks, beams, abandoned trunks, and smoking buildings, he felt he was seeing for the first time the true horror of all that had happened.

Somehow, maybe because Jackson Street had been saved, Nick had halfway expected to find other pockets of buildings that still stood or could be repaired. But block after block, all he saw was desolation—a flattened, blackened plain where a vibrant, noisy city had stood just days before.

Here and there, the ruins of a few brick walls still stood upright. Once Nick saw the remains of a steel-framed building, where the flames must have burned like a furnace, bending and melting the metal into curved, limp pieces.

Shake pattered at Nick's heels, head down. He didn't stop to sniff like he'd normally do. All the live, earthy smells dogs usually love were gone.

"We're going to Golden Gate Park now, Shake," Nick told him as they skirted a pile of broken bricks. "Tomorrow maybe we'll search the relief camp at the Presidio for Tommy. I don't think we'll find him, though. But I'm sure Annie will be real glad to see you again."

On Market Street, Nick caught sight of a small brown cap peeking out from the ashes. It looked a lot like his own. He couldn't help but think of the boy who must have worn it. Nick wondered how many people had died these last three days and if their names would ever be known.

He kicked at a patch of ashes with the toe of his shoe.

"If I hadn't met Pat, I might have been sleeping in an alley Wednesday morning. I might have been crushed by a falling wall or trapped in rubble until the fire got me," he said softly to Shakespeare. "No one would have reported me gone. No one would have missed me or even known my name."

Shake barked once and wagged his tail. He graced Nick with a wide smile. "Yes, thanks, boy," said Nick, scratching the big dog's head. "I know you'd

182

miss me. Even if you did run away and cause so much trouble."

Nick reached over and pulled the brown hat from under the cinders. He dug a hole with a stick and buried it carefully under the ashes and dirt. As he did, Nick made himself a promise. He would do something in his life; he wasn't sure what. Some small thing would do, just something so his name wouldn't be totally forgotten.

Golden Gate Park was a sea of white tents, stretched as far as Nick could see. There were makeshift shelters, too, constructed out of blankets, sheets, and odd bits of furniture. People cooked on small stoves or waited in line to get handouts.

Nick hoped he could find the tent where he'd left Annie and her mother. But he didn't need to worry. Annie must have been keeping watch. She saw him first. Or rather, she spotted Shake.

"Shakespeare!" she screamed, and charged at them, braids flying. "Nick, you saved Shakespeare!"

Shake got hugged first. But Annie gave Nick a big hug, too. She hopped up and down, chortling with joy.

"So, Nick, you've come for your quarter at last. What took you so long? Why didn't you come yesterday?"

"Yesterday? Well, yesterday I was still fighting the fire," Nick told her, grinning. "Most of Jackson Street was saved. Mr. Pat came back. He has a lot of work to do on his store, but he should be able to open again soon. But, Annie, the rooming house burned down. I'm sorry."

He paused. "How's your mother?"

"Mama is much better, although her side still hurts a lot. But of course she can't be moved." Annie leaned her head in close to Nick's. "Don't you want to know why?"

Without waiting for his answer, she blurted, "Because she and Will are being taken care of in the tent hospital here."

Nick frowned. "Will?"

"My new baby brother!" Annie clapped and bounced from one foot to the other, braids flying. "He was born last night at midnight. And he's perfectly perfect."

"Wow. So you're a big sister at last." Nick almost felt like jumping up and down himself. A baby! Safe, after that long, terrible journey.

"Mama and I decided to name him after you or Shakespeare," Annie told him. "I wanted to call him Nick, but Mama thought that might be confusing. Nick and Nick."

"Yes, I can see that." Nick grinned. "But why Will?"

"William Shakespeare, silly." Annie reached into a pocket of her dress. "Now stick out your hand, Nick. Here's your two bits. It's the very same coin."

184

"Thanks, Annie," Nick said softly. He held it in his hand and closed his fist over it. "Monday is my birthday, you know. I'll be twelve. That's the best birthday present I could have. Besides knowing you're all safe."

When Nick visited Mrs. Sheridan, she surprised him by reaching out to give him a hug. "Thank you, dear boy. You'll always have a place in my heart for what you did for us."

Nick felt his face get hot. He peered into a nest of blankets at the baby's small face. "He's sure little," he said, which made Annie and her mother laugh.

Nick brought out the small purse Pat had given him. "Your rooming house is ruined, ma'am. Mr. Pat . . . Pat says to please accept this gift and we'll do what we can to help you come back to our neighborhood once things are rebuilt."

"And you're staying on with him, aren't you? Well, I think you two will make a good team," Mrs. Sheridan said, tears shining in her eyes.

"Three," corrected Annie. "Don't forget Shakespeare."

When it was time for Mrs. Sheridan and the baby to rest, Annie walked with Nick and Shake to the edge of the park.

"I'll come back and visit in a few days," Nick promised. "And it looks like you were right. We'll be neighbors after all."

Annie nodded, but she seemed anxious. Suddenly she grabbed his arm. "Before you go, Nick, I . . . I have something else for you."

"What else?" Nick was curious. "You already gave back the coin."

"Don't be mad." Annie's astonishing bright eyes filled with tears. She reached into her pocket and then thrust something into his hand. "I found it on the floor. It just looked like such a nice family. I was so glad you went back for my picture. And so I decided to take this one with me, too."

Nick looked at what he held. It was the old photograph of Pat's family. Nick stared. "Annie, do you know what you've done?"

Annie shook her head until her braids bounced.

"You've saved one of Mr. Pat's most valued treasures."

That afternoon, as Nick turned the corner onto Jackson Street, he spotted Ed Lind standing in front of Pat's store. Ed was watching Pat put the finishing touches on a sign. It was really just a board nailed over the empty space where the window had been.

"Hullo there, Nick," called Ed. "I was just reading a newspaper article about you in the *Call*."

"About me?"

"Here, let me, Ed." Pat cleared his throat. "I've been onstage, after all."

186

---◆---

BOY HERO
RISKS ALL
&
SAVES DOG

---◆---

Nicholas Dray, of Jackson Street in San Francisco, became a hero on Friday when he entered a smoking building to rescue his dog, Shakespeare. The boy's courage was even more remarkable because he defied a soldier who mistook him for one of the looters who have taken advantage of our city's misfortune.

When asked why he would risk death for a mere canine, Nick declared, "He is a good dog. A very good dog."

Nicholas Dray is the ward of Mr. Pat Patterson, one of the city's most distinguished literary figures and owner of the stationery store Shakespeare's Scribes, now open for business on Jackson Street. Says Mr. Patterson, "All charred items, many of them still in working order, will be on sale, and new stock is expected momentarily."

---◆---

Nick listened, and couldn't keep from smiling. He was certainly not invisible any longer. Written up in the newspaper, before he was twelve!

When Pat finished, he and Ed burst into laughter.

But Nick was confused about one thing. "I don't understand—what is Shakespeare's Scribes?"

Ed Lind pointed. "Look there. It's Pat's new sign."

Nick stood back and read the words out loud:

Shakespeare's Scribes

Quality Stationers

Open for Business in the New

San Francisco

With a New Name and

Expanded Management Team

Now that you've survived
the fire and the quake,
it's time to tell the folks back home
you're safe, for goodness' sake.
So stop in here for postcards, paper, and a pen.
We've got some for women and some for men.

And if you cannot write, don't worry,
for we can fix that in a hurry.
Pat and Nick will be your scribes,
with worthy Shakespeare at our sides.

Shakespeare barked three times and grinned. He wagged his tail, his whole body wriggling with joy. Pat Patterson wrote his name on the bottom of the sign with a flourish and handed the pen to Nick.

"Sign your name, Nicholas Dray, boy hero and businessman of San Francisco."

Nick threw his cap into the air and then took the pen in his hand to begin.

EPILOGUE

One afternoon in late fall, when the air was still full of hammering and pounding and trucks and carts unloading supplies, Nicholas Dray came down Montgomery on his way home.

He was about to turn the corner onto Jackson Street when he saw a man pacing up and down the sidewalk, muttering under his breath.

To Nick's surprise, the man suddenly threw himself on the curb and buried his head in his hands. His shoulders heaved. At first Nick thought he might be drunk—after all, Hotaling's whiskey was pretty popular these days.

Nick knew that although liquor had been banned in San Francisco for ten weeks after the disaster, the stash that Ed Lind had managed to save had been sold elsewhere. It had given the company a boost. Best of all,

Ed Lind had been promoted for his extraordinary efforts in saving the warehouse.

Nick wasn't that surprised to see the grief-stricken man on the curb. For a long time after the disaster, people had been desperately seeking their lost relatives. It wasn't easy to find survivors, especially among those who had lived in the rooming houses south of the Slot.

Now the city was being rebuilt, with new businesses opening every day. Most of the relief camps had closed. Some people without homes had left the city altogether. Others had moved into small wooden houses—shacks, really—that folks called earthquake cottages.

192

Thanks to Pat and Mr. Lind, Annie's family hadn't had to live at the camp at Golden Gate Park for long. Mr. Lind had found them a room to stay in at the back of the warehouse until the rooming house on the corner was rebuilt.

Seeing this man on the curb now made Nick think about Annie's father. How she had worried what would happen if he came back to look for her! And for a moment, Nick's heart lifted. But then he realized the truth—this man was too old to be Annie's father.

Nick knew Annie hadn't given up hope that her father would come back, but she didn't talk about him so often anymore. She was busy helping her mother, for one thing. Mrs. Sheridan managed the rooming house now, a job that allowed her to take care of baby Will.

"As I climb the stairs ten times a day without any pain in my side whatsoever," Mrs. Sheridan told Nick one day, "I often think how I would never have made it out of the building without you."

"You shouldn't thank me, ma'am," Nick said. "I . . . I don't really deserve it. The truth is, I forgot about Annie that day. If she hadn't shouted for me . . ."

"Have you been feeling guilty all this time?" Mrs. Sheridan smiled. "Don't worry about Annie Sheridan, Nick. Like this city, my girl is a survivor."

Sometimes Annie, Shakespeare, and Nick walked through Chinatown. After a long struggle by the Chinese people of San Francisco, Chinatown was being rebuilt in the same neighborhood.

"Do we come here so often because we're still looking for your friend?" Annie asked once.

"I guess so. But I have a feeling he's not coming back," Nick told her. "I went looking for him at the relief camps, but I never found him. He had a dream of being a singer. Maybe he's onstage somewhere."

That's what he told Annie. But Nick knew the truth was probably a lot different. More likely, Tommy had ended up living in a home for Chinese orphans or working for another greedy relative.

Annie nodded solemnly. "Well, I'll fly to the North Star tonight and help him find his way. You never know."

You never know. Nick remembered Annie's words when, many months later, he came home to find a letter on the store counter addressed to *Nick, The Stationery Store, Jackson Street, San Francisco.*

"Hullo, my boy," said Pat, coming out from the back room, followed by Shakespeare, who jumped up and licked Nick's face. "Glad to see you're home from school. I'm just back here doing the books. Come tell me about your day."

"Hi, Pat," Nick replied with a grin. "I'll be right there."

Nick put his schoolbooks down on the counter and opened the envelope. Inside was a small newspaper clipping. He unfolded it carefully as Shakespeare leaned against him, and smiled when he saw the headline, "All-Chinese Barbershop Quartet to Perform in New York City."

Nick laughed as he scanned the article. So, Tommy had made it! He was singing in New York.

The envelope felt heavy. Something else was in there. Reaching inside, Nick's fingers closed tightly around a silver quarter. Then he drew out the other quarter from his pocket.

For a long moment, he stared down at the two shiny

coins in his hands. He had both together again, just like when he'd started out on his journey. But so much had changed.

Nick wondered if anything had changed for Rebecca. Most likely, though, she was still working in Mr. Hank's fields.

And then there was Gran. Thinking of her made his heart ache. It probably always would. Yet Nick could imagine Gran looking at him now and giving a satisfied nod. *Although,* he thought, *she'd probably want me to cut my hair.*

At that moment a bell tinkled and the door behind him opened.

"Good afternoon. I'm looking for an inkwell as a present for my wife," said a tall gentleman with a black umbrella. "Can you help me, young man?"

Nick folded up the clipping so he could show it to Annie later. He slipped the two coins carefully into his pocket.

"I certainly can, sir," said Nick with a grin, giving Shake a pat. "Welcome to Shakespeare's Scribes."

AUTHOR'S NOTE

Into the Firestorm is fiction, but it is set during real events. In 1906 San Francisco was the largest city west of the Mississippi, with a population of 410,000. The San Francisco earthquake and fire, one of the worst natural disasters in American history, began at 5:12 a.m. on Wednesday, April 18, 1906.

Today we understand more about how earthquakes occur than people did at the time. The top layer of the earth is called the crust. It's made of several thin and rigid pieces called plates, which move and push against one another. As they do, weak spots or breaks, called faults, may develop. When pressure along the faults builds up, the plates jerk and slip, releasing waves of energy that cause the shaking that occurs in an earthquake. The San Francisco earthquake occurred along the San Andreas Fault, which extends about 290 miles along the California coast between the Pacific plate on the west and the North American plate to the east.

Although the earthquake caused major damage to buildings, the worst destruction occurred from fires. Many began as a result of open gas mains or faulty stoves. One of the largest, called the "Ham and Eggs Fire," broke out shortly after the earthquake on Wednesday morning when a woman began cooking breakfast, unaware that her stove was damaged.

The city's firefighters fought valiantly. San Francisco had a professional fire department of about six hundred firefighters, with more than three hundred horses to pull fire equipment. But the firefighters couldn't control the flames. The fire alarm and telephone systems were down, and many streets were blocked by rubble. And while there was water in some of the reservoir systems, firefighters often couldn't make use of it because the earthquake had ruptured underground water mains and other pipes. Since the firefighters couldn't get water flowing through their hoses, they used dynamite to create firebreaks. But because the dynamite was often used incorrectly, instead of stopping the fire, it caused the fire to spread.

As the fires spewed huge plumes of dark smoke, thousands of people took refuge in city parks in large tent cities. San Francisco lost most of the downtown area. By the time the fires were finally controlled on Saturday morning, 28,188 structures and 508 city blocks, or 4.7 square miles, had been destroyed. During the disaster, soldiers patrolled the streets with orders to shoot looters.

For many years, the official estimate of the number of deaths was about 450. Collapsing buildings probably caused most of the deaths. Now, however, thanks to the efforts of city archivist Gladys Hansen, it is thought that about three thousand people perished.

Into the Firestorm was inspired by a story I came across while researching the disaster. A boy named Charles Nicholas Dray had run away from a county poor farm and been taken in by a local merchant just a few days before the fire. Left alone while his new employer was away on business, Nick braved a soldier's gun to rescue business records and his employer's dog, a retriever named Brownie.

I decided to set the story on Jackson Street, near Hotaling's whiskey company and government offices called the Appraisers' Building. This was one of the few downtown areas that survived the fire. Today it is a historic district filled with charming old buildings, art galleries, and antique stores. The cashier for Hotaling's, who really was named Ed Lind, left a fascinating eyewitness account of how the neighborhood was saved.

The character of Tommy is also based on an eyewitness account. Fifteen-year-old Hugh Kwong Liang lived in Chinatown at a time when Chinese people faced much discrimination. Abandoned by his cousin when Chinatown was evacuated, Hugh escaped the city to live with a distant relative and eventually pursued his dream of becoming a singer and entertainer. After the fire, efforts were made to prevent the Chinese from returning to their old neighborhood, because it was in a desirable downtown area. After an international protest from China, residents were allowed to return and rebuild.

There are many books, photographs, and Web sites about the San Francisco earthquake and fire. Here are just a few:

For pictures and eyewitness accounts, including one by author Jack London, visit the Virtual Museum of San Francisco at www.sfmuseum.org/1906/06.html.

Gladys Hansen and Emmet Condon's book, *Denial of Disaster: The Untold Story and Photographs of the San Francisco Earthquake and Fire of 1906* (San Francisco: Cameron and Company, 1989), contains many rare photographs of the disaster.

Books for young people include *Quake! Disaster in San Francisco, 1906,* by Gail Langer Karwoski, illustrated by Robert Papp (Atlanta: Peachtree Publishers, 2004), and Laurence Yep's *Dragonwings* (New York: Harper Trophy, 1977).